❧ *The Widow*

SUSAN YORKE

The Widow

HARCOURT, BRACE AND COMPANY   NEW YORK

To Enrique

The Widow

CHAPTER ONE ✍

I had always known and had been waiting for the realization (and rejecting it when it came) that my penalty for having what I considered a neat, unemotional life would be the uncomfortable forfeit of being obliged to love a man younger than myself. My projection of the story was incorrect, for I invariably imagined myself as a sprightly matron of seventy with a flare for some pink-cheeked youngster of twenty. I should have understood that I had not that much time to fritter away, and that my story would be concentrated, significantly enough, in the period that I had chosen as a child to represent what I liked to term my "ripeness," my fortieth year. You were exactly a decade my junior, but even one day or one week, or one year would have sufficed to fulfill the requirements.

You, your history, your private affairs were all known to me for a considerable time before I met you. You entered my life as a name some three years before I held your hand in my own in the conventional gesture of greeting, welcoming you, among other guests, to my house and garden. In the gossip that had surrounded you at that time I had taken your side without cause or basis. When people had asked me if I knew you I had been uncertain what to reply, for of course I knew you without ever having seen you or spoken to you so I usually answered:

"Not exactly, but I know *about* him."

I was not foolish enough to ignore the meaning of these frequent encounters by proxy with you. You were much talked of, which signified you were somehow distinguished; we talk of people as a rule when they puzzle us by behaving contrarily to what we have expected. I do not believe that meetings between two people are preordained, but I do believe that a series of accidents conditions us to wish to meet a particular person and eventually our wish leads us to an occasion where it can be gratified. The speculations about you which took place around me, and the sum total of gossip, remarks, criticisms that I heard or eavesdropped to awakened in me an awareness of you. I did not consciously plot to meet you; but I knew that I would miss no opportunity that might guide me to a meeting with you. As it happened, you came to me.

One day I was shown a photograph of you in sports clothes standing with a group of people I did not know, laughing and relaxed in the sun. "There he is," I was told; "the second from the left, the tall one." I remember thinking how strange a mechanical apparatus is that it can evolve, as a camera does, the witchery of a likeness and this likeness be exhibited months or years later in a distant place to people entirely outside of one's life. Although you were *of* the group you did not give the impression of belonging to it; your clothes differed from your companions' as if you were fighting to assert your individuality, your smile had none of the insipidness of the standard snapshot smile. You were like a player in a stage role, possibly an agreeable role but still a well-acted part and not reality. You stood out from the group and the film faithfully registered this distinction.

Through the constant chatter about you, the somewhat racy anecdotes told concerning you, the photograph I had been shown, my interest in you increased so that you became a kind of secret hobby of mine, if I dare put it that way. That I had an intuition you would have, some day, something to do with me is understating my reaction. I knew that I must learn about you so that I should be well prepared to meet you; I did not know, and could not at that time suspect, what I would have to do with my knowledge of you.

When I learned, much later, that you were coming down

from the mountains to live in the city where I continued to reside even after my second husband's death, I understood that the inevitable occurrence was at last about to take place and I was curious about the future. Your story and mine were nearing that point where they would fuse—for a while —into one story. I was not impatient, for I suspected this story would be important to my life.

You sent me flowers the day you first came to the house, roses that arrived early in the morning, and with them was your card addressed to me in your slanted, angular writing; my name, in brief, written by you, a supposed stranger. It was significant that our first communication was a written one. In the Bible it is insisted: "In the beginning was the Word and the Word was God," and then later, in the New Testament, it is written: "God is love," so it requires no juggling to see that in the beginning was the Word and the Word was Love.

In that instant when I first saw you I understood, without accepting, who you were going to be to me. Indeed, it was obvious at once; I sensed it and looked closely at you to see if I could detect any disquiet on your part, and I thought I could. At the same moment there sped across my mind the thought of, or the essence of (for *thought* is far too pro- longed to indicate what happened) the two episodes, years apart, which I now realized were preparations for you. At such a time, the mind seems to open and swell and enfold many scenes which it nevertheless keeps distinct and un- blurred. It is as, when one enters an art gallery, the eye sweeps over twenty paintings in a second, seeing them all without difficulty, but studying none.

My first intimation of you was when I was a child summering with my cousins at Blankenberghe, a Belgian seaside resort near Ostende. We formed a clique, my cousins and I, and ruled the beach, inviting or rejecting other children to our exclusive circle. There was only one child who eluded us by the very fact of honestly being unconscious of us. She was a tall barefoot girl who moved quickly over the sands clothed, as we all were, in brief bathing trunks, chest tanned by the sun, dark hair cropped close. I don't recollect her name, only that she came from Luxemburg and stayed at the same hotel as I. Her brother, younger than she, belonged to our group but never spoke of her nor endeavored to introduce her. She was perpetually busy by herself, digging clams far out on the stone quay, wading in the late afternoon in a special search for star-fish, or building, as the tide receded, elaborate sand-castles. At lunch-time she would call her brother from a distance in a peculiarly flat voice that was somehow melodious and just faintly nasal. Her parents obliged her (as mine obliged me) to wear a dress for luncheon on the hotel terrace, and I remember my mother observing what a crime it was to let the Luxemburg child sit in the sun in such an expensive Italian silk print. All her dresses were of imported silk, whereas mine were of ordinary cotton, but she seemed unconscious of this mark of wealthy distinction. In addition, instead of being sleeveless as mine were, her frocks were long-sleeved. The sea wind used to billow out the silk from her arms and slap it against her; the material was forever

13

straining away from the tight cuffs at her wrists as if anxious to take flight. It was an inexplicably tender and satisfying picture to see her seated at lunch with the wind playing about her dress and hair, her clear eyes looking abstractedly out over the water, the even, white teeth flashing in the dark face as she smiled when her parents spoke to her. Sometimes our glances met and she would smile at me, somewhat self-consciously, but frankly friendly. To us, as a group, she never paid the slightest attention, and some warning that encroachment on her privacy would lead to disaster kept us from the invariable, inescapable teasing that children inflict on any of their number who is "different." She was in Blankenberghe two summers in succession. I saw her daily for a total of four months and I never exchanged a word with her, although I watched her as often as I could and thought about her a good deal, mostly in pictures. We had no need, apparently, to talk to or to touch one another; our mutual presences were sufficient for each of us, plus, of course, the shy smiles we were willing to bestow occasionally upon each other. There was no sequel to this story, and not until ten years later, while attending the university in New York, did I discover what this child from Luxemburg meant in my life and so, in turn, realize on meeting you why I had remembered her through so many years.

It was a hot summer day when you came that first time to the house. You hurried to me (later I was to realize you always hurried and there was seldom any necessity for it, you liked speed for its own sake) and in the moment of reaching me, hung back a bit, as a child does on being introduced. I was obliged to look up into your face, and I found that although the photograph had recorded you accurately enough it had failed to convey the atmosphere in which you wrapped yourself; you marshalled a series of expressions across your bony, predatory features; first you charmed me, then you examined me, then you obeyed me and at last you left me. All this you managed, with extraordinary mobility, to put across to me in the interval of a few seconds. You controlled your features as a theatre manager controls his props. It was not that you belied the photograph, or even the accounts and comments I had already heard about you; it was rather that in intensifying everything you rendered them incomplete, unsatisfying, even untrue.

Measuring you as you stood before me, I sensed a hidden rivalry in you against myself and the life I represented. You obviously were well accustomed to being the center of attention, and surely you understood immediately that in my house and in my circle *I* would demand the title role. Possibly you thought there was room enough in my way of life for two leading characters. At any rate, I was at once aware of the latent competition you harbored beneath your fine exterior.

You loitered on the terrace waiting for me to take the initiative. Behind you the swimming-pool glittered in the strong sun. I remember I said to you, evenly and almost mechanically:

"Change into your bathing suit right away and be comfortable. The dressing-rooms are over there," and I pointed to the ivy-covered bath-house at the far end of the pool.

What made you leave the door open while you took off your coat, I don't know, and how I happened to be in the only part of the garden from which it was possible to see into the dressing-room, I don't know either. You stood in your shirt sleeves, fussing with your tie, when you suddenly seemed to remember the open door and in the moment you turned to close it, a hot erratic breeze billowed out the thin material of your shirt so that only the tight cuffs anchored it to you. I felt, diffusedly, that the picture was significant, but it was only later that I connected it with Blankenberghe and my childhood. Blankenberghe, looking back upon this whole story now, had been a kind of prologue hinting at what sort of play my emotional life would be; a late episode at the university was the first act setting the stage, indicating and preparing for the entrance in the second act, of the main character, yourself.

The element which most disturbed me, that first day with you, was your familiarity. You were, of course, distant, reserved and meticulously polite, but everything about you was somehow already known to me, the shape of your mouth, your habit of sitting with the palm of your hand covering your lips, the timbre of your voice, your quick, jerky movements, the expressions of your eyes. Although I knew positively that I had never seen you before, my mind kept insisting, "Of course you have seen him before, of course, think where, think where."

All this took place beneath the outward show. We exchanged stories, accepted second cups of coffee, smoked cigarettes, moved our chairs deeper under the myrrh trees to

escape the sun. I doubt that even the most perspicacious onlooker could have detected anything more than a normal
lazy Sunday afternoon group digesting in the cool of the
garden, preparing for another dip into the pool and some
further tennis when the court should be shadier.

Yet it was precisely during this innocuous initial conversation that I realized my link with you. There seemed to be
between us a kind of *humming,* I can give no more accurate
description, so that whatever you said, or did, never jarred
me but flowed into my thoughts or ran parallel to my actions. It was never necessary for me to ask you "What did
you mean by that?" or to frown at you—as I've frowned
at countless guests—for a misplaced action or a stupid observation from which, like a good hostess, I must make the effort
of gracefully extricating the culprit.

My awareness of you sharpened as I relaxed deeper into
the cushions of the chair; my energies concentrated in this
amorphous non-physical field leaving my body still and undisturbed. Slowly I became conscious, as I studied you, of
the importance of touching you. I don't mean that I was
assailed by any violent desire to touch you; on the contrary,
it didn't even occur to me to do so for I was preoccupied
with the *idea of,* the *significance of touch,* not with the fact
of touch. I understood that *if* or *when* I touched you, the occasion would be important. With you, I knew there would
be no meaningless encounter as I distributed tennis balls or
fetched extra rackets or handed out towels or served beer;
this casual touching of hands that often occurred between
me and my guests could not occur between you and me

simply because nothing that we would do in relation to each other ever would be casual. You had avoided any accidental nearness to me during the afternoon, and by exactly such a trivial non-action we entered our first understanding, established our first contact.

As a rule, thinking back over one's life, one is apt to do no more than remember certain outstanding events. It is rarely indeed that one is driven to any analysis of those events or to any consideration of the significance of one's past actions. When the present is full, or agreeable or exciting, there is no temptation whatsoever to probe into the past except to pull out amusing vignettes for the entertainment of friends over cocktails and at dinner parties. I don't honestly recollect what thread started me examining my past, but I do not doubt that it was closely connected with you. The past, slowly, seemed to be asserting itself in the present.

My lawyer—an elderly gentleman who methodically administered my widow's financial affairs, a trusted friend of my deceased husband—brought you now and then to my house to play tennis with some energetic weekend houseguest or as escort for some grass-widow or spinster for the Saturday lunches in the garden. I looked forward to your coming, I enjoyed drifting to the court to watch you play, I was pleased to glance down the long table and see you. You were very quiet, speaking little, and you had a bad habit of slouching in your chair at the luncheon-table and paying a minimum of attention to the babble of the ladies to your left and right. I suppose after the years you had spent up in the mountains this kind of life was strange to you and you were gradually acclimatizing yourself to it. I tried to be especially considerate of you, for I was acutely aware of what life is in the mountain mining camps and I knew, from my own experience, how radical are the adjustments to be made in the unimportant things when one comes out of the adobe huts of the altitudes and the roughness of the mines into the sophistication and luxury of a large city. I tried to put you at your ease and thaw you out before others, but you were shy in company and the mountain coldness seemed still to hang about you as if it were a protective mantle. Perhaps you did not wish to relinquish the one weapon that the isolated mining-camp life gives— the ability to be alone and self-sufficient—without first acquiring another, somewhat more suitable to the gregarious metropolitan life.

I was waiting for you to take down your barriers and talk to me. You would talk to nobody else and yet you experimented here and there with various young women as if anxious to make sure that your path lay nowhere else, that it was proper for you to come to me. You reminded me of an animal who knows that his food awaits him at a certain designated place but detours to arrive there, and sniffs and scratches along the path, postponing his arrival and at the same time making sure there is no sustenance elsewhere. I knew of your young women, they varied every few weeks, and mutual friends told me of your doings, what restaurants you frequented and with whom, what sort of an apartment you had, what brand of whisky you served, with whom you went horseback-riding on Sunday mornings. I received incredibly detailed reports about you from many sources; I was a passive detective agency, for I never asked about you.

Furthermore, it was obvious that although you might enter into my life, I could never enter into yours. What practical place could I have in the life of a young bachelor? You, on the other hand, would always find a place in the house of an older widow who entertained a good many people including other juvenescent bachelors considerably less interesting than yourself. Youthful bachelors, to phrase it brutally, are essentials for a hostess; in addition, my old lawyer was grooming you to replace him in the office and it was only natural you should come frequently either with him or substituting for him to discuss business problems with me. But what conceivably respectable place could an attractive widow have in the public entertaining scheme of any bachelor?

Scandal accumulates easily about vivacious personalities, widows and the wealthy, and, qualifying on all three counts, I automatically exercised care in deportment with everyone, especially with men. The advantages of physical attractiveness are more nonchalantly carried off by the young than by the middle-aged. Any woman of forty is conscious of her good looks, if she has any, and experience has taught some of us to observe care in how we exploit our own charms.

Beyond your life in my house there lay, as yet untested, still another life, yours and mine together away from my house, away from people, away from the social tags of *widow* and *bachelor,* away from the business and the tennis. This was to prove the dangerous point of our relationship, not in a moral sense but in a human sense, for in this life together we were to find unsuspected obstacles within ourselves to the natural, dignified living of it.

I had known you only a few months when I decided to touch you. This happened, prosaically enough, during a walk to the local cinema. You were at that time entangled with the daughter of a political acquaintance of my old lawyer's, and he, of course, did everything in his power to further the attachment. Perhaps it is wise to state here that my old lawyer had a peculiar attitude towards you compounded of jealousy mixed with need. Being himself a gross, flabby man, he resented your contained and muscular figure but at the same time was happy to exhibit it as one exhibits a pedigreed dog even though one is oneself but recently come out of the gutter. Half-blind and of owlish habits, he naturally found your keen sight and delight in sports a nuisance, and he liked to complain you "weren't serious enough." However, he was a sufficiently shrewd business man to estimate your value both to himself personally and to the firm, and so he suffered your attacks of gaiety, your youthfulness and your eternal entanglements with what grace he could call up on those days when ulcers made the mere act of living unbearable. He frequently observed, watching you gobble your food for the sole purpose of nourishing yourself, that you had no sensitivity towards the fine things in life and then he would toy with some undigestible delicacy that had him belching and retching for the rest of the day as he alternately chewed and puffed his cigar.

In brief, my old lawyer thought your flirtation with the

girl a good thing politically and I, without any conscious reason, was opposed to your becoming intimate with anyone, no matter how good a "connection" for the business such an intimacy might turn out to be. I privately and not too charitably considered as an enemy this daughter of my old lawyer's life-long friend but refused at that time to be so blunt in my evaluations and decided she was merely a socially ambitious girl who thought your height and tailor and disarming smile were what she needed in a husband, for of course these attributes would make you a conspicuous and envied figure in the city's drawing-rooms and so secure for her additional invitations to ever more exclusive homes. You were an above-average escort and it never occurred to her that the society chatter of select drawing-rooms might bore you.

As we walked, you discussed this across me with my old lawyer, complaining that your feet ached with standing at cocktail parties, that your ears rang with the shrillness of women's voices, that your eyes smarted under the inescapable cigarette smoke, and that the assemblies, in the summer heat, invariably sweated and stank like so many horses. As we stepped from the curb to walk in the wide, deserted tree-lined street, I slipped my left hand through your arm and fell into step with you. Your arm was completely tense under my hand, stiff and unyielding, even unfriendly. It was the very unnaturalness of this rigidity that told me at once you wanted my hand on your arm, that my gesture was pleasing and important to you. You treated your arm as if it were a frail bit of precious porcelain temporarily in your possession and being grossly misused by a boorish amateur who might break it. I enjoyed that unrelaxed, protesting arm under my hand, but it was, nevertheless, over a year before I repeated the intimacy. You had shown me, more clearly than in a written contract, that you were as aware of my importance to you as I was aware of yours to me. I could afford to take the time to know you better, to study you, to learn your tastes, your reactions, and, most necessary of all, your weaknesses. The deeper and fuller emotional associations are, the more apt they are to disrupt and destroy those who experience them. I had no intention of foregoing the pleasure and education of such an attachment; but neither would I permit myself to be destroyed.

I began, in brief, to hunt you; not as women hunt the men they wish to catch and marry, not even as animals stalk the prey for when they are hungry, but as a killer hunts the victim, for there was no doubt that the coming relationship between us could not wind up in the normalcy of marriage, nor could it descend to a repetition of the usual procedure in the common love-affair—we were not primitive enough for that—so what other course was open? One of us had to be the victim, and since I was the first to recognize our importance to each other, the first to make an active move— that of touching you—I took for myself the right of deciding how the roles we must enact were to be distributed, and so I made you the victim in order to save myself, my way of life and the happiness of the people concerned with me. Had you had the choice, you would have done the same.

At my age I had learned to identify the symptoms that

precede a sentimental or emotional attachment and I had also learned how dangerous such affections can become. My mind at once indicated that it would be ludicrous for me, a widow of forty, to attempt to marry a young man of thirty for love alone; you liked and were too well liked by women for such a marriage ever to be a success. I should have entered, by marrying you, the kind of hell-and-torture which would age me even more rapidly than nature. I should die a dozen deaths daily through justified jealousy. My mind also showed me that in a love affair with you I must logically be the loser; I had everything to teach you and there was no subject in which you could instruct me. What could a youngster of thirty, fresh out of the mountain wilds, teach an urban widow of forty? And yet, whatever cord or bond existed between us was sufficiently powerful to force me towards you but yet to seek some sort of relationship which would remain under my control. Before ever undertaking it, I realized only too clearly the long fight my mind would wage against my instincts. My mind was able to save me, my instincts could only destroy me.

There is, actually, no such thing as chance; the future must irrevocably be a direct outcome of the present which is, in turn, rooted in the past. There was, then, no chance that we might escape each other; because of our characters, our own desires, we were obliged to come together; we were already responsible for the conclusion of an episode not yet begun.

CHAPTER TWO

*L*ike most people who do their daily tasks rapidly and easily, I am extremely slow and patient in any undertaking which requires long-term planning. In executing trivial problems I am hurried and concentrated; in the two or three big issues that have so far occurred in my life, I have been diffused and even non-active. The ripe moment, when it comes, insures a ripe action, and any forcing of a situation invariably produces a muddle.

Perhaps this philosophy is reflected in my physical appearance. I have often been called "cold" very likely because, having in common with most women a very sensual nature, I hide this by affecting trim and unusual attire so that attention invariably centers first upon my clothes and person and only secondly upon my face where the clever can read my weakness in my eyes and the curve of my mouth. As a kind of atonement for this streak of naturalness in me, this desire to be constantly, irresponsibly close to nature, I have imposed upon myself the duty of taking a strong and controlling hand in the law firm which my second husband left me when he died. Law is nature's worst enemy and so I have taken a certain satisfaction out of squeezing from the law such handsome profits that I can gratify any material wish I might entertain.

Because of my seeming concern over the law firm I have been termed a good business woman, and because I have always dressed with exceptional luxury, I have been considered fashionable. As natural corollaries, being considered a good business woman I am thought to be intellectual merely because I am educated, and being fashionable I sometimes mislead people into describing me as beautiful.

We found, you and I, that we had similar tastes in books and music and you fell into the habit of bringing me presents of both when you came to the house. I began to learn more about you through your choice of records to play on the gramophone, through the books you wanted me to read.

Around town we seldom met; the life of a young bachelor in a large city would hardly throw him into the same sets frequented by an older widow, furthermore I had small interest in nightclubs and bars, preferring the comfort of amusing myself and my friends in my own home. There was one notable exception: concerts. Only during the winter was any good music to be heard in town and then not much of it, so that the circle of music-lovers—and the city's elegant society who wished to be seen in cultural pursuit—met repeatedly during the "season" in the opera-house where the majority of the concerts were played.

Opera-houses in metropolises are the same everywhere, heavily gilded and lushly carpeted and highly dignified in an abundance of burgundy plush. The city's opera-house was really the epitome of all opera-houses, larger than New York's Metropolitan and, although not so pleasing, certainly as elaborate as Paris' Grand Opera. I usually took orchestra seats in preference to boxes, and I preferred to sit rather far back in the house, from which vantage point it was always possible to see not only the stage but the audience and to comment to whoever accompanied me on the concert-goers as they dawdled up and down the wide center aisle during intermissions exhibiting their hats and furs or the good-looking girl clinging to their arm.

You generally sat further forward than I, and in the dim half-light of the concert I usually could see the back of your head or, in the intermissions, watch you discuss the program with whichever young woman you had brought to keep you company. You rarely went alone; the fear of finding no one to speak to probably kept you from that for, at all costs, you

27

never wished to appear an outsider, although it was always obvious you were one.

Above the red plush seats, set in the dome of the opera-house roof, there is a decorative rounded frieze of composers' names. I don't recall when I first noticed the frieze but I know that it was because of you that I looked at it. It had become suddenly an impossibility to observe you any longer, and, seeking for a place to rest my eyes where the movement of the conductor, the speeding violins, the intricate coiffures of the women and the nervous headshakings of the men would not distract me, I looked upward. I could as easily have gazed down at my shoes but that would have been, in a way, inconsistent with my character, for to stare down is an indication of hopelessness and to look up is an expression of striving. Discovering the frieze, I naturally immediately associated it with you. I read the names carefully: Verdi was in the middle; and spreading out from him to the right were Meyerbeer, Wagner, Debussy, Mendelssohn and Weber; and to the left, Liszt, Chopin, Brahms, Beethoven and Puccini. What was opposite I could not see, for only half the circle was visible to me, the other half closed over my head. Then I watched you to discover if you ever consulted the frieze as I did, but you did not. I knew that some day I would ask you:

"Have you noticed the frieze in the opera-house? Why do you suppose they put Verdi in the middle?"

In the meantime, that frieze was a consolation and a safe-guard. It provided me with a perfect place to look whenever, in the many concerts at which we both assisted, I found it unbearable to observe you.

In a sense I have done you a partial injustice, for you did attend the opera-house concerts alone several times but only when you knew I would be there. I used to smile when you came to my seat at intermission to discuss the music; you were so serious about the minor faults or merits, and I knew this seriousness was simulated, partly to impress me with your knowledge of contrapuntal composition, polyphony and the rest, partly to keep up with well-informed musical friends of mine, and also—although this you could not at that time admit—to seem to remain on the safe surface of an ordinary relationship while sending out feelers into the profounder side of our future association. I am no musicologist but, unlike most others of my generation, I have had the good luck and the money to hear music all my life under the world's ablest conductors and through repeated hearings I have come to choose how I personally wish to hear a particular passage. When that passage is not played my way, which happens often, I nonetheless *hear* it my way. Romain Rolland, in his *Jean Christophe,* in speaking of Beethoven, has his hero remark that he never heard bad music because even when music was poorly played he *heard* it, within himself, as beautifully played as it should be. Your critical faculties, by which you were attempting to save your emotional life from upheaval, could not permit you to hear the music within yourself; you forced yourself to hear it from the outside. It was an act indicative of almost everything you were doing with regard to me during that period. When you relaxed your vigilance over yourself and slipped inward you went to extremes to regain the comforting superficiality;

you criticized with great detail, or you simulated non-interest, off-handedness, even boredom; you concocted a litter of lies and strewed them unconvincingly in my lap.

I loved those afternoons and evenings of concert time in the opera-house, comfortable in the red plush, surrounded by superbly dressed plutocrats who neither had contact with nor interest in the music they were obliged to hear in exchange for the opportunity of exhibiting themselves. Nothing ever intruded upon me during these hours. I was all ears, soaking up the fine sounds like an expensive sponge, and considering you. I can't say I thought of you, for music impedes thought; rather I *felt about* you, which is what I mean when I say I considered you. I imagined no love-scenes between us, I invented no stories about you, I merely felt and enjoyed my contact with you across the intervening rows of seats, for I knew, beyond any doubt, that you were also aware of me. I had no wish to offend this awareness; I was satisfied that it existed; you were nearing me. You were as conscious of the atmosphere of the opera-house as was I (although not yet forced to the necessity of consulting the frieze), you were hearing and yet not truly hearing the same music as I, you were skimming, like a cautious skater, around the thin ice that covered the whirling depths of our joint future. That last inner resort of yours, the core of you, such as it was, which I planned to attack, had scented the danger I represented and was already fighting me, although the upper layers of your conscience, your many preoccupations with this girl or that, with your career and your comfort, lay like a damper on all that was below and ignored the struggle deeper within.

This entire episode in the opera-house was familiar to me, for it was an intensification of what already had happened to me in the university. Ordinarily, speaking loosely, one could call it a repetition, but it was so much more profound than its original, because I myself was older and possibly a bit sharper in my awareness, that, although the outward setting was almost identical, the inner results were quite different.

The scene in the university had been laid in the campus chapel where, at six o'clock every Sunday evening, the head professor of the music department played the organ for an hour. He had a predilection for Bach and I learned the works of this master through four years of steady weekly attendance, the only times I ever entered the building of my own accord. In winter the chapel was illuminated by the same dim half-lights that I was to see years later in the opera-house of this city. I sat far back, not snug in furs but bundled in the regimental polo-coat that every college student considered an indispensable part of her wardrobe.

I came early and scrunched up in the corner of the pew, watching the broad entrance portals, for I was waiting in that feverish expectancy which indicates a complete lack of judgment of whatever object arouses it. When she entered, in a kind of lumbering walk, I always was breathless with sheer excitement, for it seemed to me incredible that anyone so lovely, so inconceivably glowing and beautiful could yet be what I considered so evil, so weak, so false. It was not the

Lesbianism itself which I considered evil; on the contrary, I dismissed that with an emancipated wave of my hand as "so much glandular trouble"; it was the kind of life she led which I found so inexpressibly evil, and the abnormal future composed of constant criticism and resultant subterfuges. I erroneously believed, in those formative university years, that a valuable person must express herself honestly and that that honesty must be, somehow, within the prescriptions of society. Her weaknesses and falseness were one and the same thing; she lied, she twisted, she was unreliable, and, worst of all, she tortured. She lacked the stamina to say, "I am different, I'm going to do things my way, take it or leave it, I don't care about you." As a consequence she had a positive genius for inflicting upon herself and anybody in contact with her the most exquisite and unnecessary mental excruciation. Possibly she found in such anguish an expiation of what she no doubt considered her sins and faults.

But who among us dares to say "I am different"? We strive, all of us, for insignificance (we call it "conforming") and yet secretly would prefer to be outstanding. We are wretchedly afraid of actually being so, for outstanding is synonymous to unorthodox. Unfortunately, unorthodoxy terrifies us more than mediocrity. In mediocrity lies security; the unorthodox—the dissenters, the leaders and frequently the saviours of civilization itself—receive, as a reward for their being "different," the smoke and flame of the stake, figurative or actual.

She sat diagonally opposite me in the chapel, hunched in her corner of the pew, facing me. There were few students who cared for Bach and the audience at these organ recitals was composed, as a rule, of not over thirty or thirty-five girls, isolated and, by tacit understanding, seated as far apart from each other as was physically possible. Rarely did a pair attend, or a group. All the misfits and hyper-sensitives of the university came, licked their wounds in private and gobbled up strength for the coming week to oppose the mob, the teachers, the conventions. We had an unobstructed, if indistinct view of each other, she and I. And I studied her then with as much carefulness (if with less talent) as I later was to study you, for I was anxious to break down the defences she had built up against me, I wanted to know I could possess her to the last hair of her head, and I insisted upon the satisfaction of driving her to unrest because of me. She saw me, and rightly, as her enemy, for I was attacking her integrity. Unless I could be the victor over her *in my way* I could hardly realize my own potentialities; my development would have been checked young and very likely my emotional life would have grown into something abortive and cramped. Throughout our lives, we grow and flourish at the expense of our victims.

Her case was different from yours in that, being of my sex, she could recognize the enemy whereas you could not; you saw only the loving mistress. Unlike your attraction to me, or mine to you, hers for me was entirely physical. By the time *you* began to question yourself whether you "wanted" me in any but a physical sense, I had insured that you would have to discover you loved me for many attributes and qualities which were *not* physical. With her, I gained her interest and subsequent enmity by insuring she would want my company for discussions, assistance and admiration and then permitting her to find out for herself that that was merely a blind, what she wanted was purely and shamefully physical, that she needed the warmth and tenderness of bodily love for her own quiet and repose. The discovery shocked her.

She would sit with her dark head inclined—even that is a similarity, for you often adopt the same pose—and dart quick glances at me when she thought I might not be looking. How many times have I caught you looking at me in the same way, never, of course, "catching" you openly, as I "caught" her, but by watching you in a mirror you had forgotten existed, by observing your reflection in a glass doorway or against the crystal of a picture or even in the quiet, undisturbed water of the swimming-pool.

Sometimes we walked out of the organ recital together, she and I, the edges of our coats barely touching.

"What did you think of it?" I would ask, not because her opinion mattered a damn, but for the pure pleasure of hearing her voice.

She usually smiled when she spoke, a means of disarming me, I imagine, and yet, at the same time, the half-apologetic grin of the weak person. She had an extraordinarily perfect mouth; I once found it reproduced in a Picasso painting, a mother and child of his early romantic Blue Period; her teeth were even, strong and brilliant ivory. She betrayed herself, her antipathies and desires, by the expression of her mouth, exactly as you did, and like you she enacted her comedies and pretences with her lips. The mouth is the en-

34

trance to the being, to the soul itself if one cares to be poetic, and I made it my business with you, as with her, to know every expression, every contortion of the lips that either of you could summon into existence.

"Well, of course, he's wonderful," she might answer, side-stepping as was her habit, speaking of the music professor instead of the music.

It was her voice, vibrant yet flat, almost unnoticeably nasal, that made me recognize in her the Luxemburg child from the Blankenberghe beach. Here again was the same short-cropped dark hair, the same clear, abstracted eyes, the same withdrawal from everyone into a private cell, the same concern with self and with individual, unshared amusements. We had gone beyond the clam-and-starfish hunting but it was just because I was attempting to intrude upon her privacy that she treated me as an enemy set to rob her most precious possession, her loneliness. I wanted her, as all lovers want, to share herself with me, and that was a surrender she fought against. What right, indeed, had I to intrude upon something exclusively hers? I loved her flat, low voice; she spoke, as it were, in a perpetual minor key. Now and then, as if trying to show how normal and carefree she could be with me, she used to force her voice into exuberance, and it would rise a bit, shrill, and burst forth: "It was perfectly *aw*-ful," she might say, and you felt her lungs would burst if she prolonged the word "*aw*-ful." Years later, I heard the same exaggeration in your voice.

What inner alchemy renders us always susceptible to the same charms? I could never claim I had been unaware of

35

the danger inherent in the specific voice so pleasing to my ears, or of the tilt of a head or the sameness of certain expressions, and I suppose my whole life I will seek just those requisites in whoever will be close to me, always as the incurable adventurer seeks danger, but a *known* danger, when he explores new territories. The adventurer who penetrates the jungle will scarcely be he who travels the following year to the Arctic. Aware of the ambushes, the climate, the tricks, the storms, the fevers and the reward, I veer consistently to one type of person, and the fullest expression of that type was yourself.

Who were you, what were you? How long have I watched you, catalogued you, analysed you and loved you in order to obtain the answer! And the answer known, in so far as it can be, of what importance is it? I can explain you as a botanist can explain an unusual plant and, like him, I must leave the luck of my finding and the *fact* of your existence unaccounted for; how can the peculiar arrangement of traits and talents in you be fathomed? They only can be recognized, as the veins and chromosomes of the plant; it can be said they are as they are because of specific anastomoses which automatically give a predicted result, but the *why* of these combinations is inexplicable.

In you I uncovered, first of all, a great deal of myself, more of myself than I wished to find, and that made my penetration of you much easier than I expected. In turn, you recognized our similarity but you were, in the beginning, too concerned with yourself and your problems to evaluate its significance. I used the similarity as a weapon for, through myself, I knew you; I needed to be only disconcertingly honest with myself, a difficult and often disagreeable business. You were, also, similar to my dead husband, a lighter, more volatile stamping from the same mold, the town where you grew up, your career, your ambitions and those slight, unconscious movements we each make which reveal our nerves, all these were as my husband's were. When studying you or examining an action of yours, I could not interpret it through self-knowledge, I was able to explain it through knowledge of my dead husband. With this double-edged sword, how could you escape me?

Did you not even instinctively—for you never knew him—copy my husband in details, in the type of shirt you bought, in the embroidering of your initials over the heart, in the materials of your suits, in the quality of your socks, in the manner of knotting your tie? Through this, you presented a well-disguised and even enviable front to the crowd, and people like us—outsiders—have bitter need of an unblemished façade. And did you not sit like my husband, with your right ankle crossed on your left knee, your right elbow propped on the arm of the chair, your hand hiding your mouth in that gesture that has been a part of my life? What should I find strange or unfamiliar in you who blend so well the being I love best in my life, myself, and the being whom I have valued most, my husband?

Perhaps I have mentioned too precipitately that we were outsiders. However, that was one of the strongest ties between us. We were foreigners deliberately entered into a new land before it was actually necessary to flee the old one.

We had read the handwriting on the wall. The old country had no opportunities to offer to such as we. I was in a relatively safer position than you as I had neither race, creed nor religion against me and my passport was valid and incontestable. You, on the contrary, had every disadvantage that the political world has to date devised; when you wished to travel, visas and permits were difficult, even impossible, to obtain because of your race and birthplace. So much was closed to you—public careers, voyages of exploration and pioneering, places to establish permanent residence. You came of pure, civilized blood, and because of it were impersonally persecuted. On the other hand, I come of mixed bloods which have bred restlessness and which have driven me to immigrate as potently as if I had been, as you, politically forced to do so. And immigrants, to whatever country, in whatever century, are invariably drawn to each other, reaching out for support and assistance, for the roots have been cut from beneath us and we have not yet been able to grow leaves above our heads to shelter us from tempest.

It was in Paris, during a temporary pause in my unending travels when I must have been fourteen or fifteen years old that I took the exceptional resolve to make a strength and a virtue of being an outsider. I would emphasize, wherever I went, not minimize my foreignness; I would fit in and be tolerated—if never actually accepted—everywhere *because* I was different, never because I was insignificant or "the same as everybody else." I had been to twenty schools in as many countries and I knew, down to the last mortifying detail, how the foreigner is made to suffer if he endeavors to en-

croach upon the privileges of those who have already established themselves, the ex-foreigners, as all are everywhere in
the world, eager to forget that once we, too, had no place
where we belonged. As a result of my Paris resolution, I was
often in demand, for people bored with themselves or their
provincialism or both welcomed the novelty I provided. I
made it a rule to abandon a place before this newness became stale; my blood drove me to seek change and I had
the good fortune to exhaust what those about me could give
me before they exhausted me.

Our bloods, yours pure and mine mixed, led us to the
same city at the same epoch; we could not have survived
elsewhere.

Your pure blood had been perfected through countless
decades, your people have devoted themselves to honored
professions, have lived well and quietly and, until the wars of
this century, have flourished and multiplied, secure, established and protected in one of the oldest cities of the world.
You were so civilized, so cultivated and so decadent that you
carried within yourself your own destruction, and your over-
educated intelligence warned you of this; you were unable
to escape into ignorance. You had within you the ability to
be the finest expression of what man could be would he not
make war and wreak destruction; but you would never be
allowed the opportunity to develop as you should in order
to realize this expression. You were drawn to your own destruction, seeking it out with unerring skill, battling yourself to death instead of your fellow man.

Significantly enough, your family have been healers for

over five hundred years, doctors from father to son. Is there greater generosity and greater forgivingness than to heal?

Both you and I come out of the bourgeoisie, and by that I do not mean anything disparaging. The bourgeoisie which produced you was probably bourgeoisie at its best and that which produced me bourgeoisie at its worst. In using the word I am not concerned with an economic class struggling for the ownership of the means of production, but with a standard of living and a way of life. There is usually a stigma attached to the words "middle class" when, in reality, the middle class should be lauded as that group which, under industrial capitalism, came closest to recognizing, however theoretically, the golden mean between aristocratic ostentation and underprivileged misery. There may be justified contention about the moral rights of the middle class to its golden mean, for example, my own monetarily ambitious family, frankly out to leave the golden mean far behind, and by judicious skinning of the sucker, crash the gates of millionairedom. The successful execution of this philosophy early demonstrated to me that very obviously all men are not created equal; some are decidedly cleverer and more unscrupulous than others. From the paddocks of the bourgeois field in which I grazed, I saw all society as bourgeois; the successful ones had become aristocracy, either monied or titled, but aristocracy in a world of bourgeois standards, and the unsuccessful constituted a dissatisfied segment of society termed proletariat. *Your* bourgeoisie, the professional classes more interested in medicine and law and science than in financial returns and social privileges, seldom crossed my path; and when I inadvertently encountered members of it, the education of my family and friends caused me to refer to such beings as idealists—a more refined way of saying crackpots.

I have detailed our economic-philosophic backgrounds merely to show that I come from a bustling, active, practical and certainly a moral setting and as a consequence was able to execute with relative ease my schemes involving you, whereas you came from a restrained, passive, impractical and almost religiously moral seclusion and so fell a prey to me without even being aware of your perdition. That your background is the goal of reflective, civilized and thinking man, and mine of this century's greedy human animals, is beside the point. It is perhaps more pertinent that you fell victim to me, that cultured man lost out against materialistic, accumulative woman.

CHAPTER THREE

Much later in our relationship, seated beside you one day in the opera-house, listening to a Strauss concert directed by an imported conductor, I noticed that, in the intermission, instead of conversing with my friends or me, you jotted down on the glossy program what looked like comments.

"What are you doing?" I asked you curiously, for you were so absorbed in what you were writing that you did not even raise your head to watch the parade in the center aisle, a diversion you generally did not miss.

"Oh," you answered, scribbling on, "I'm just writing down notes on the concert."

"What for?"

"For my father," you told me; and then, because I must have looked so astonished, you explained to me that you and your father exchanged comments on all the concerts you each attended in the different cities where you lived, and that each concert either of you heard was duly criticized on the program itself which was then immediately mailed off.

"How long have you been doing this?" I asked you.

"All my life," you answered casually, and made hiero- glyphics opposite the *Don Juan* which had just been concluded amid frantic applause. You passed the program to me and I deciphered your cryptic observations slowly.

That was again one of those moments when half a dozen different threads of my life fused into one and I seemed to be holding a finished, strong cord in my hands. My first reaction was one of envy; *how wonderful,* I remember thinking, *to have a father with whom one maintains this kind of contact.* My own father, true to his kind of bourgeoisie, had *used* music as a cultural achievement; I suspect he found a certain relief in it, but he never savored it, never enjoyed it, never left it alone; he manipulated it. Concert-time or music served a purpose for him, either social or emotional. My mother liked to sing the romantic arias of certain operas she had heard, as a young girl, from her family's box in the opera-house of her native city every Wednesday and Saturday evening. The *Berceuse de Jocelyn* and "Depuis le jour" from *Louise* were her favorites; both pieces make me nervous. Between the musical needs of my parents, I had grown up as a heretic. I treated music as one of the natural things in my life, somewhat like sunset or dinner, and I admired or criticized, as occasion demanded, without any real emotion. I needed music as much as I needed sunlight and food; I never considered it possible to do without it. Very likely this was one of the contributory factors that drew me to you rather than to some golf-playing, jazz-mad member of the kind of bourgeoisie in which I had been brought up.

I had learned rather late in life that people *shared* music, as you were doing with your father, for example. Until my first marriage, I had always considered all music as exclusively mine. My first husband, a man of many social talents and a phenomenal memory, turned out to be a novice to music, a fact I found rather more amusing than irritating. It never occurred to me to initiate him to music; on the other hand, I had no intention of forgoing music because of his lack of interest and I ordered a gramophone and records along with the rugs and draperies and living-room suite of our first home without thinking twice. To test the gramophone when it arrived, I played the first record that I unwrapped from the packages sent by the music shop; it happened to be Strauss' tone-poem, *Don Juan*. I listened closely merely to make certain the machine functioned properly, and it was with surprise that I noticed a rapt, somewhat sheep-like expression on my first husband's face. He was "discovering" music; to his social talents he was adding that of being a music connoisseur. He adored the *Don Juan* and spoke of it as "our" music; whenever he wanted forgiveness for some offence, when he desired to establish a mise-en-scène for a game of loving, when he wished to create a certain mood, he resorted to the *Don Juan*. He played it so often that our friends and acquaintances came to associate the piece with him and, in the gregarious way people have, guests would fumble through the record collection and extract some bit of music, everything from *Porgy and Bess* to a Bach toccata and fugue and assure me that this was *their* special piece of music. It was because of these revelations that I again turned to Proust's *Du Côté de Chez Swann* and analysed every sentence written about the "petite phrase" in the sonata of Vinteuil. My mind understood exactly what each rounded, perfect, Proustian sentence meant, it made supreme sense, it was accurate, searching, even surgical in its precision.

Ces charmes [I read attentively], ces charmes d'une tristesse intime, c'était eux qu'elle essayait d'imiter, de recréer, et jusqu'à leur essence qui est pourtant d'être incommunicables et de sembler frivoles à tout autre qu'à celui qui les éprouve, la petite phrase l'avait captée, rendue visible.

In a less exquisite sense, that was what they were all doing, the first husband, the guests fumbling through the records, you writing to your father: recapturing. I did not understand why there existed the necessity to return to the past to obtain a drop of satisfaction or pleasure; it seemed to me the present was the only time, in so far as *time* can be said to exist at all, worthy of my consideration, and by *present* I meant also the future implicit in it. This *Sehnsucht,* this yearning, this melancholy for what was gone was to me so much eyewash, entirely false, even hypocritical, something on the same scale as attending the cinema—one projected oneself into a celluloid situation and wept and agonized through it as if one were the protagonist. Why did humanity insist upon the recapturing of some item of the past? I did not for one instant believe that this recaptured item, the inspiring, associated incident, had been as tender, as significant, as enchanting and moving as the music connected with it. And why was the present so dissatisfying that humanity ran like dogs for cover in a rainstorm to the shelter of the unalterable past? I accepted as a fact, without understanding it, that most people wish to live with their pasts, always provided, of course, that this past has then been so spiritualized, improved and generally beautified that it has lost almost all semblance to actuality.

The past, to me, is dead. It is a perpetual corpse that one carries about and generally it stinks like anybody who rots. Everything I am, or know, in this moment is the sum of what I *have been;* therefore, what need have I to modify and distort episodes? The past is to be looked at impartially, as one looks at the corpse, and no resurrections should be expected. Had humanity then so little confidence in its ability to enjoy the present that the present was never considered as good as the past?

At any rate, I learned that almost everyone shares music and, experimentally, I tried to share it too. I made a violent attempt to enter into the *Don Juan,* I battled and hacked my way into it. It was the old story of everybody being out of step except Casey, and I was reasonable enough to see the fallacy of this. As Casey, I made a hop-jump and tried to fall in step with my first husband and his friends.

When, a year later, we were transferred to a post in South America we had some four months of constant travelling and visiting and calling during which time I never heard the *Don Juan*. We attended concerts and musicales in the drawing-rooms of several national capitals, ate ices and petit-fours while somebody interpreted Chopin on an Embassy piano, caught snatches of symphonies while driving about in other people's cars with the radio turned on, but the *Don Juan* never crossed my mind; I had forgotten about it.

Unpacking together our belongings in the new house, puffing in the high altitude of this unfamiliar post, we put away the record collection in special shelves. A native electrician played with the wiring of the electrical phonograph and finally signalled to us that the machine would work.

"What shall we play first?" I was asked.

I was about to make a careless reply ("Anything you like, dear. . . . Whatever you feel like hearing, dear. . . . Whatever's nearest at hand, dear") when something in the tone of voice caused me to look up from the floor where I sat cross-legged in a litter of wrappings, albums and records and met my first husband's eyes. I understood at once that a special answer was required; I am a poor guesser but patient enough at deduction and, after a pause which was simply uncomfortable for me but apparently fraught with significance for my first husband, I had the tact to produce the correct reply.

47

"The *Don Juan,* of course," I said, and wondered how many marital disasters are averted by just such a hair's-breadth of hesitation.

He played the *Don Juan* to everybody who came to the house. The consensus of opinion was that it was sexy music.

Some six months later, realizing tardily and not understanding at all, worried and desperate at the failure of the marriage, he sought in the eternal "let's fix it up quick" male manner to "win" me "back" by taking a long, romantic trip together to the southern lakes of a neighboring country. Is there indeed any marriage that, sooner or later, does not reach that point where the husband, looking one day at the wife and finding everything somehow wrong, does not offer to take her "away from it all," "to start over again," "the second—or fifth—honeymoon," "just us two alone together, darling." And is there a husband who does not say to his wife, when she requests a divorce, "Oh, you women don't really know what you want; you are nervous; I'm sure you can't have made up your mind about this. Think of all we've been through together; think of the children; think of this, that and everything else, and be reasonable. It will pass. I won't get drunk again (not right away), I won't take the blonde out again (not this week), I will be more generous about money (just for a month)."

We travelled through barren, impoverished country until, after three days, we came to the lush vegetation of the southern lakes. The railroad line ended, surprisingly enough, at a most modern and unexpectedly elegant hotel, streamlined and chromium-plated from its bougainvillea-covered terraces to its cork-ceilinged bar, overlooking an improbable perfect cone-shaped snow-covered volcano rising from the opposite shore of the quiet lake, exactly like the invariable Japanese landscape of Fujiyama.

Tired and dirty, we arrived at night; the air was warm and soft and wet, it was mid-summer and the wind came from the tropics. A page-boy led us down wide, carpeted halls, around innumerable corners, and finally paused before a pale, honey-colored pine door. We followed him into a square room hygienic with modern furniture where one wall consisted of French windows that opened out upon a wide terrace overlooking the lake. I walked to the terrace to escape the scrape of luggage and clink of coins awarded as tip; behind me I heard the door close and then the rapid steps of my husband approaching me. There was an annoying moon that looked like a stage prop, and the lake shimmered exactly as it should have to satisfy the most exigent movie-director. And in that hundred-per-cent romantic moment the latest and most inescapable of the hotel's modernities was exhibited; a loud-speaker, connected to an electric phonograph (which I subsequently found situated in the bar) produced, suave and dulcet, the *Don Juan*. Somebody had mixed the sequence of the records and the throbbing wooing phrases coiled in the lovely night without the blaring preamble of the opening bars, insinuating themselves on the senses, almost gooey with over-expressed sentiment.

Without any effort of will, I stood outside myself and watched the scene. It reminded me of countless cigarette and deodorant ads; he and she and the moon and the lake, and now, as a crowning touch, sound-effect too. Irritated at my own lack of response I told myself earnestly: "This is *our* music. This is the *Don Juan*. This we've heard together all over the world. This means something. *Our* music." My dutiful repetition of "our music" had the unfortunate effect of at once reminding me of a favorite passage from Aldous Huxley's *Brave New World* in which is described a scene where soft amplifiers repeat certain phrases all night long into the subconsciousness of sleeping children. ". . . and Delta children wear khaki. Oh, no, I don't want to play with Delta children. And Epsilons are still worse. They're too stupid to be able to read or write. I'm *so* glad I'm a Beta."

Our music; *our* music; *our* music.

I felt the hand on my shoulder, heard the shaken voice near my ear and I tried to respond. Perhaps, I speculated, I don't know what I want; perhaps there is no such thing as feeling; perhaps there is only thought; perhaps thinking is feeling; can you *think* being tickled?

Whoever was managing the phonograph apparently discovered the mistake about the sequence of the records, rectified it, and the *Don Juan* burst out with its opening clamor, trumpeting and shrieking. It beat against my ears, evoking not the slightest shred of response. In desperation against this lack of reaction I distinctly remember saying to myself in concern,

"My glands aren't working properly!"

"Darling," whispered a voice next to my face, "this is *our* music," and, entirely beyond the possibility or even the desire to explain, I sank, according to innumerable stage-directions, into anxious waiting arms and hoped the embrace would not last long as I had not been to the bathroom in eight hours.

Sharing music, I decided, was a trap that one person laid for another, a subtle means for binding the beloved, a hold that one person tried to wield over another. I reserved this knowledge for future use, privately doubting I should ever have the cheek to practise it.

"What did you think of the *Don Juan?*" you asked me as I returned the program to you. The lights were already dimming in the opera-house, there was that settling-down, last-minute nervous rustling of programs as the audience composed itself comfortably for the second half of the concert.

What, indeed, did I *think* of the *Don Juan,* and how phrase it concisely before the conductor came to the podium, raised his baton and galloped his orchestra into the next musical stretch. What did the *Don Juan* make me *think of;* *that* you might well have asked with more point.

How explain to you, to whom all music was emotionally linked with somebody or something in your past, that I associated the *Don Juan* with urinating? How try to tell you that I connected it with my first husband without its having had any romantic significance in my relationship with him? How convey to you that I had listened to today's performance of the *Don Juan* without noticing if the guest conductor had been faithful to the score or had inserted his own interpretation? How inform you that music, any music, was indivisably mine, if I chose to accept it, and that I would comment on it and discuss it no sooner than I would comment on or discuss my lingerie.

I felt you looking at me in the half-light, waiting for my answer, expectant, certain that the *Don Juan* must mean something to me, that I would tell you and that you would understand me better as a result. Your male urgency was suffocating me and inexpressibly tiring. Give an answer, give an answer, I told myself; I felt as if I were drowning in blankness and inarticulateness. In the instant before the conductor tapped for attention on his frail wooden stand prior to raising his arms above the heads of his orchestra, I leaned towards you and gave you, in dramatic sotto-voce, a reply that I thought would please you.

"It always reminds me," I murmured, "of my first husband."

I could feel you relax in the plush next to me, exuding satisfaction.

I was made aware of your colossal, complex-riddled vanity through an incident at one of the numerous concerts we attended together. A world-famous pianist gave a recital that was at once, traditionally, both a social and musical event, and the old lawyer thoughtfully reserved a trio of excellent orchestra seats beside (and slightly below) the lush box of the city's leading socialites. He wished to be seen with me and he was sufficiently generous to include you in his scheme —that was his business astuteness, for, after all, some day you would have to rope the clients in to him like so many fatted calves and he planned that you be seen with the right rich people, that is, with reputable wealthy widows such as myself.

The socialite family was so many, so overburdened with its own offspring that it occupied, actually, two boxes. As we seated ourselves I nodded a greeting to them collectively and the old lawyer bowed politely in homage to society's gilded leaders. You did not know the clan and I sensed your permanently uneven temper ruffling in protest beside me. I noticed, casually, that the family's only beauty—they were a thick-jowled bunch on the whole—the family's only beauty, the imported, titled wife of one of the younger heirs, had decided to accompany the tribe in the prolonged absence of her husband in Europe. She was exquisitely dressed and her exotic veiled and feathered concert hat was easily the most noticeable bit of flippant haberdashery in the house. I leaned towards the old lawyer, who was staring at the beauty with frank, appraising delight and observed:

"Helena looks charming this evening."

"Gorgeous, gorgeous," he breathed back.

Of course you overheard.

Exactly when, during the concert, I noticed your flirtation with the beauty I am not sure. I think my attention wandered from the acrobatic arpeggios because I felt you looking at me at too great a length. When I turned to reprimand you I found your eyes focused *beyond* and *above* my head; in the concert semi-dark you were carefully seeking the answering look of the beauty. Then I saw the bait you were offering and I was divided between shame and laughter. I might have pitied you had I not known how much you abhorred pity. You were literally exhibiting your hands, you held them in the childish "here's-the-church-and-here's-the-steeple" formula; your elbows were propped on the arm of the seat and you could flex and unflex your long fingers with a minimum of disturbing movement.

Annoyed that I had caught you looking towards the box, you stared fixedly at the pianist, but you continued with the display of your hands, unconscious that I had penetrated that trick, too. Your hands have always been your pride and, clumsy and inept though they be, they are nevertheless magnificent hands, exciting in their perfection. Watching your fingers stretch and relax my thoughts veered, as no doubt the thoughts of the beauty also veered, to the pleasures of sexual play, for you were so obviously hinting: "Imagine these hands on you; think of the delight of these fingers on your breasts and over your loins." I frowned and moved uncomfortably in my chair and you threw me a quick, interrogatory glance. Then you understood that I had seen through your intentions and your hands plummeted into your lap; you laced your fingers tightly together. Out of the corner of my eye I saw your lips fold stiffly. I believe in those moments you hated me, my vigilance and my unfailing awareness.

At intermission the beauty left her family's box and as soon as you decently could you excused yourself and hurried out to the lobby to join the fashion promenade and seek an encounter. On a higher economic level, this was an execution of the village promenades where the maidens, arm in arm, circle about the town green and wait for the swains to pluck up the courage to approach them.

Leisurely, strolling beside the old waddling lawyer, I followed you, curious to discover if you had had any success.

I came upon the scene just as the beauty, separated from the clan, inadvertently and adroitly dropped her cigarette and you were able to supply her with one of yours and with what an irresistible mixture of the roué and the shy adolescent. Your bold eyes expertly examined her plunging décolleté, her wrists, her ankles, and yet you held yourself in an innocent schoolboy's attitude. You smiled and spoke to her in a low, intimate tone, and she replied. I watched your conquest, wondering what dissatisfaction in her private life drove her to seek distraction in this way, wondering if you really were so seductive that women gravitated willingly to you.

The old lawyer and I returned to our seats without waiting to see the conclusion of your play. Just before the lights dimmed the beauty entered her box and then, streaking in excited haste down the aisle, you came and slipped, flushed, into your seat beside me. During the second half of the concert your hands remained inconspicuously in your lap and you never once looked towards the box. Under cover of the applause that concluded the recital you whispered to me, bending over me,

"You'll value me more when I succeed in things like that." Then you looked at me with that peculiar, lucid, unblinking stare that was meant to indicate your earnestness, and you added, oddly enough and more accurately than I could have anticipated, and with a certain unexpected bitterness, "What else can you value me for?"

You had correctly estimated, in this instance, my inner reaction, but I was surprised you had taken the trouble to tell me.

CHAPTER FOUR 🖋

The first time
we drove together in a ramshackle taxi to your apartment,
skidding and slipping over the wet streets, you told me that
nothing in the world was ever new to you, everything was
eternal repetition, and the older one grew the less one even
sought to find new things. It was impossible, you claimed,
ever to share anything with anyone after a certain age. You
compared man's emotional capacity to a theatre in which
there were so many seats—a limited number—and, with

each succeeding year, the number of empty seats—seats not occupied by the association of a bit of music, a line of poetry, a particular scent, a certain locale with somebody held dear —decreased until, finally, the whole theatre was full and there were no more seats to dispense.

It struck me as a strange analogy, this desire to treat the people in your life as an audience watching the main actor, yourself, entertain them from the stage. Perhaps this is, after all, as most of us treat our emotional experiences if we are rich enough to have a full house of them. A greater exhibition of egocentricity could hardly be conceived.

I looked at you curiously, for I considered it odd that, on the threshold of knowing me, you should define our coming relationship as a mere repetition of your former liaisons. Such an inflated vanity fascinated and at the same time repelled me. Obviously you were wrong, for the conclusion to our relationship was going to be new to you, if not the relationship itself.

Is there in this world anything more interesting, more entertaining, more satisfactory, more varied than two people? Why, then, were you so concerned with only the one? There is nothing duller, more monotonous than one person, unattached, undirected, lethargic, savoring everything, tasting nothing, seeing everything, understanding nothing. It is the linking up, the becoming two that produces the exciting new and joint personality.

Possibly you hoped through your preoccupation, your *obsession,* with yourself to become a being worthy of attention. But the more you peeled off this layer and that, the better

to arrive at yourself, the smaller you became, like the onion
in the *Peer Gynt* legend, the onion that was patiently peeled
for the secret in its core, but there was no secret, for the
onion consisted precisely in its peelings and with the last
peel the onion disappeared. The core was invisible, a nothingness enclosed in the last two peelings, very much like the
frequently spoken of and equally invisible soul of man.

An old uncle of mine used to tell me that people were
like vegetables; some were turnips who hibernated pale and
white, some were carrots who burrowed down under and
blazed fire-like only when dug out, some were corn reaching upward to display themselves, some were wheat swaying
in whatever wind, some were peas locked up in a shell and
very small when finally discovered, some were asparagus,
unable to live without finicky assistance, some were rice,
demanding to be trampled upon. When you weren't being
onion, you were being pea.

Of course, your shell was your greatest asset. You gave
the impression of being quiet, reserved, disciplined and self-
assured. When you had come to the city you had bought expensive clothes which flattered your otherwise gangling body
and made you look appealingly tall instead of disquietingly
undernourished. You cultivated a healthy-looking tan as a
mark of leisured distinction. You used seven toothbrushes at
a time to ensure a movie-star's denture. You rehearsed expressions before the mirror and played them out, the
charmer, the offended, the irate, the wounded, the light-
hearted, the heart-breaker, the little boy. You had your
photograph taken and a flurry of prints made for distribu-

tion to various admiring young women, front-face (for your nose was too hooked and predatory to ensure a flattering profile). You were, in a word, physical vanity incarnate as a compensation against the intolerable doubt within. You garnished the shell until it shone in splendor, until it was irresistible, and within was the agonizing emptiness, the long hollow in which you were a miserable, protesting little pea.

You wanted to be a leader without the discomforts which leadership imposes. Is there a man alive who does not dream of leading a battle, or a diplomatic mission, or a country, or a financial program or an artistic innovation? And who does not reconcile himself to his slippers and the evening paper because leadership is too strenuous, too consuming, a business for adventurers and the super-ambitious?

Your intelligence aided you to develop in the shelter of the pod, rather a bigger pea than most, but inevitably you had your moments when you needed somebody who would kneel before you and so you were obliged to pick, as a consequence, people weaker than yourself. The easiest prey was, as a rule, woman. You asserted, lectured, moralized, whipped and tortured until you had reduced some half-pint adversary to a snivelling mess of tears. Then, confronted with the physical evidence of your manly superiority, you generously "forgave" the disgusting scene and kicked the little lady out. You could be a contented pea for another two months.

The half-pints, by a curious twist of fate, invariably crossed my path; their existence was living, clamorous proof of my necessity to vanquish you or join their ranks.

"Please try to understand," you said to me once as we lay together, "I don't want to hurt you. I don't want to be thoughtless and careless. But I am exclusively and entirely preoccupied with myself."

To be preoccupied exclusively with oneself is the surest method to court misery. One is never what one wants to be. One can twist, turn, contort, but within one remains an undersized pea. To visualize oneself as one should or could be is to approximate the position of the thirsty desert traveller who sees before him Fata Morganas of water, the convincing mirage forever unattainable.

It is true, naturally, that—with the exception of some rare souls—we place ourselves first, we are each of us walking, talking Numer Ones, but we are not everlastingly concerned with ourselves as *personalities*. We are concerned, rather, with our success before a specific problem, with the new clothes we buy, with eating food commensurate to our diet, with keeping appointments and catching trains, with kissing the girl and lifting the cheque off the man.

Turning towards you, I found you looked deceptively innocent as you lay back on the white pillows; you looked at ease, unspoiled and delightfully, alluringly young. Surveying you now from within the angle of your arm, I was reminded of young Joseph in Genesis, the perfect youth, the intelligent, calculating seducer, the irresistible, clean boy who was most assuredly, somewhere in your remote genealogy, an ancestor of yours. That you lacked his ambition, his lust for power and glory simply enhanced your attractiveness to me. In my fondness, I placed you above such con-

61

siderations while I knew (when I thought without the fog of love) you were incapable of realizing an ambition or of wielding power.

Always, when I was with you, I succumbed to your charm; your physical presence was a sort of opiate that made me see all your virtues and blinded me to your faults. The power of your presence was undeniable. If I had planned, for example, to be angry with you or to scold you, the mere sight of you coming across a room towards me, your eyes shining with pleasure, was sufficient to make me change my mind and to receive you cordially.

Warm and content against you, I wondered what you were thinking, what this whole play of sex signified to you (if anything at all beyond an afternoon's amusement). I hesitated to ask you, afraid you might rebuff me and that, after I had been so close to you, would have been unbearable. You heard me take a breath to speak and then, as I remained silent, you asked:

"What is it? What did you want to say?"

This sensitivity of yours was so disarming that I asked at once, shortly and a bit more harshly than I wished,

"What's sex to you?"

In the instant between my question and your answer, all sorts of possible replies raced through my mind, you might say you wanted to possess me, you might say you wanted release, or you wanted diversion or you wanted enjoyment. The infinitesimal pause you made before answering worried me into thinking you resented my having asked you something so very personal. I had not yet understood you well enough to know that the more personal the question the readier you were to answer it.

"Sex is my self-assertion," you said finally.

"And does *that* make you happy?" I pressed.

"Happy!" you echoed impatiently. "What are you talking about?"

Like Joseph, having everything and pretending poverty, lolling in a veritable bath of happiness you claimed you knew nothing about it. Quietly, I slid away from you and went to dress, taking my time. You did not hear me re-enter the room and I found you still in bed, sitting up with your head buried in both your hands in the classic attitude of mourners. I stood watching you, waiting until you should feel my presence, but you sat unmoving, a figure of woe in a posture of tragedy. I suspected you were peeping at me through your fingers, they were splayed across your eyes in such a way that you could have done so, but I could not prove my suspicions. I waited until, after a few minutes, you sighed and dropped your hands and looked across your bedroom at me. Knowing what a consummate actor you were, I could hardly accept unquestioningly as genuine your expression of surprise and astonishment. In fact, I thought of your excellent, scholarly education and wondered if you were not perhaps making a deliberate exhibition of the famous adage that *post coitum animalum triste est.*

But perhaps your expression was genuine? If so, I had blundered in on you in a highly private moment and then perhaps this indicated that sex was not as much of an expression of yourself and your strength as you had pretended

63

a few moments before. If it was not genuine you nevertheless made a heart-rending picture. In every mistress there is a good deal of mother, and to come upon the man one cherishes when he has obviously let himself go, when he looks as he feels, tired and helpless, is something to make the most restrained woman fling caution aside to pamper and pet and soothe.

Painful experience had taught me, however, that such abandonment only placed me at your mercy as you would be sure to strike out at me in some way, endeavoring to get even with me, as a means of asserting yourself over me.

Instead of rushing to you, as I wanted, and granting myself the luxury of holding you, I waited for you to make the first move. Discipline is never easy and I struggled to hold myself quietly and to keep my face blank. The moments when we measured each other across the room seemed interminable, a bleak stretch of uncomfortable time out of which I had to emerge the winner. I knew with an absolute, deadly certainty that this was a sort of test of ourselves, of our relationship to each other. Although I had just "given" myself to you, this instant, which was the more important of the two instants, I was forcing my will on you so that you would be obliged to "give" yourself to me. When suddenly you held both arms out to me, smiling, in a clear invitation for me to come to you, relief flooded through me, rooting me still a little longer to immobility.

No matter how many embraces one accepts, there is always one which is particularly outstanding, an unforgettable one that becomes the symbol of all embraces. Such was this embrace of ours in which we did not speak and in which at last we found some measure of peace and understanding instead of the grasping clumsiness of unsatiated passion.

"Are you never happy just to be with me?" I asked, resuming our former discussion.

You considered, frowning, and then said,

"It's not so much happiness as satisfaction."

I couldn't find much difference between the two words.

"Happiness," you went on, pursuing your own thoughts leisurely, "is simply an escape, and all escape is illusion. There's really only one escape, one final one I mean."

I must have tensed against you because you looked down at me and asked:

"Does the idea of death bother you that much?"

"Well, death is so—" I hunted for a suitable word—"destructive," I finished inadequately, not meeting your eyes.

"So then you think only nature is destructive, and not man?" you asked, tightening your arm about me.

This was a bad moment for me and I examined my red lacquer fingernails rather carefully before I answered, and then I said that man *should not be* destructive but possibly destruction could sometimes be justified, for instance when undertaken by the individual for the self-preservation of the individual, as in medicine where the amputation of a leg might save the entire body, or in politics where the elimination of a tyrant might save a state or even in human relationships where one person could only live if his oppressor died.

As the afternoon waned and the young, rainy twilight came into the room, we reverted again to the matter of possession. I suppose we must have been talking, as all lovers do, about ourselves and inevitably we circled back to this subject. I believe I asked you why men were always so concerned with possession. I distinctly remember your reply. Your were almost vehement.

"How do you think we can avoid being concerned with possession?" you asked me, and continued immediately without waiting for an answer. "It's forced on us by our women! By our mothers and governesses and schoolteachers and wives and mistresses; a whole procession of unending female I-want-this, I-want-that, get-this-for-me, get-that-for-me. In the end, what else can we do except simplify and we ourselves *possess* this creature of boundless appetite, this being who is made up of regular complexes of possession?"

I had moved away from you during this tirade and now you reached for my hand.

"Who possesses *you?*" you asked, flexing my fingers absently in your own.

"When?" I countered. "Today or yesterday or last year?"

"Now."

I was about to answer "you" when you relinquished my hand and leaned back against the pillows, switching on the lamplight and looking at me from a slight distance and, as the physical contact between us ceased to exist, I was able to reply in full truthfulness.

"Myself."

Sitting in silence beside you, I began to think back. In the university, I reflected, I had been possessed and possessing, for there I was dealing with a being of my own creation.

66

You, on the contrary, existed, all too real; I saw you every day, or spoke to you over the telephone, I spent long hours over weekends with you, I knew your tastes, I revised your work, I placed my hand on your thigh when you drove me in your car. In the university I had created a personality out of the girl who came to the Bach Sunday-evening concerts, but whether my creation had anything to do with what she actually was, I don't know, but I seriously doubt it. Nobody could have been as wonderful as I made her; I day-dreamed her if she were not in sight, but I possessed her because what I loved in her were the traits with which I had endowed her. Nobody, save me, found her beautiful, exciting, desirable, unusual, so obviously I was in love with my own conception of her. I made her lovable and glowing because I *willed* her so.

With you I had gone on to the next step; I loved *you,* not my conception of you, for it was possible for me to see you clearly, if I chose to; and deeply as I loved you I nevertheless (in my more rational moments) criticized you. I loved you despite your imperfection; at the university I had demanded perfection and, not finding it, had invented it. With age had come a certain tolerance of, if not perpetual blindness to, the faults of the beloved. It is my misfortune to have been able to have seen you without distortion, to have had the intelligence and the will to recognize your faults and weaknesses and, loving you, to forgive them because I could use them against you. Only when I retreated into the haze of physically loving you could I forget them and pretend them out of existence, and even then it was not so much an

67

ignoring as a postponement of realizing them. I took a perverse pleasure in being able to love you in spite of your shortcomings, in loving you for what you were, of whatever stuff you were made. I never lost the ability to criticize you; the more I loved you the sharper were my criticisms, possibly as a safeguard against my own mounting passion, possibly out of a lifelong habit of criticizing. Nor were you ever able to hide your faults from me: I seemed to possess some kind of fabulous X-ray insight where you were concerned. I was able to understand you, probe your weaknesses, analyse you, and still, above and beyond my meticulous understanding, was my love.

CHAPTER FIVE

About this time you acquired a friend, a young boy several years your junior whom you mentioned frequently and casually in conversations but whom you never exhibited. At first I dismissed this boy as just another of the various people you were picking up in a big city, and I am not sure when I began to scent danger in the friendship. The friend became, to me, an annoying gadfly; he was always on hand for whatever pleasure you wanted, be it tennis dates in your club, lending you a

69

car, lunching with you when I unexpectedly broke an engagement, buying theatre tickets for you when you had not time to secure your own and, as a consequence of these multiple everlastingly obliging activities, I termed him *the stooge*.

The stooge was the kind of son every man would like to have: well-built, friendly as a puppy and generally liked, good at all sports and made for the club-life and locker-room man-to-man talks. Not yet corrupted by experience, he wore his good looks without the self-consciousness that would inevitably descend upon him in maturity; he had a generous nature that did not mind being taken advantage of, and he swam in waves of newly acquired money that his parents poured over him with the tacit agreement he should not bother them. They paid him, to put it crudely, to be obliging and inconspicuous, and some atavistic sense of decency, totally lost to his elders, made him fulfill his bargain with scrupulous attention.

You claimed this boy was the perfect antidote for you; you explained to me he "soothed" you because he was so natural and uncomplicated, such a fine, healthy young animal, brimming with good nature and health and plenty of ready cash. He had no nerves and no moods and this was balm to your jumpy disposition and your kaleidoscope succession of tempers. When I attempted to probe more deeply into your loyalty towards this blond-haired athlete you admitted to me under the vow of greatest secrecy that the boy was unhappy with his parents and you were trying to fulfill the function of an elder, helpful brother.

"He's so essentially clean," you would emphasize earnestly, "that I want to be of use to him. He needs someone. I'm not good for much in this world, but maybe I could help him."

The truth was you pitied his unhappiness and at the same time enjoyed it, for you saw that youth and beauty and money (he had all three in greater quantities than you) were insufficient to obtain tranquillity and fulfillment out of life.

A kind of blind impulse propelled me to find an immediate foil for the stooge and I began systematically to search for a wife for you. I thought a new woman in your life might eliminate the new man. I did not admit that the motivation of my search was rebellion, and a desperate rebellion at that, against the one safeguard men have against women—a fast friendship with another man. Rather, I told myself that this secondary *reason* (that I wanted a wife for you) was the only reason. I was certain that, in this necessary prolongation of our relationship, you would need, at some point, the normalcy of ordinary love-affairs, and I chose to select for you (and thus insure her harmlessness) the girl you should use on a short-term basis. If, by lucky chance, you decided to marry this girl—or, more accurately, if I decided it was to my advantage to have you marry her—that indicated that she would be no hindrance to our relationship *after* the marriage but be, instead, even a reason to deepen it. If you married a woman I chose for you, and would hand to you, as it were, trussed up delectably like a roasted piglet on a silver platter, then you would be obliged for the rest of your life to remember me because of your wife. If you married, in brief, my first modest crime, a sin against the rightful intimacy that must exist in a successful marriage, would be committed not merely without trouble but with approbation. Short-term love-affair, or marriage, came, in the end, to the same thing: I needed a woman to annoy you so that you would appreciate me the more, and at the same time I needed her as a whip against the stooge.

There was, of course, yet another angle that figured prominently in my concern over a suitable wife for you: the matter of my good name, a name that had to be protected from the inconveniences of scandal, and I felt that with you married or engaged to be married a possible discovery of our intimacy would be discredited. As a divorcée from my first husband and a widow of my second I could not afford the luxury of gossip to augment my publicity.

In brief, this girl that I sought for you was to serve me in three ways: as an antidote to the stooge; as a protection, a façade for my own activities; and, lastly, as an evidence to you of how much superior I was to any other woman you might find.

Accordingly, at parties I left the company of the men— which I enjoyed—to examine whatever unattached young girls were present; a job that thoroughly irritated me. The young girls, I found, were either too fat or too thin, too short, too stupid, too conventional, too sloppy, too tied-to-mother to fill my bill. I began to detest young girls with their virginal twitter and hot eyes, their posturings and snobby talk. And always, at the back of my head, was the knowledge that the stooge was driving me to this wretched examining and discarding. It is almost alarming to view, dispassionately, the maidenhood of the specie, and I began to admire the blindness of poets and movie directors—blindness or crassness, I could hardly decide which—that was able to present girls in any but an unpalatable light. Sweetness and charm, innocence, freshness, eagerness, what ridiculous words these were when applied to the gilded youth of the well-fed city. *Seek and ye shall find* I told myself, in reality addressing the stooge.

Sometimes I saw the stooge from a distance, once I passed close by him in the street. Although he knew my name, he did not know my face, and you were entirely unaware that I knew him by sight and that I was sending out feelers, through acquaintances, to report to me what he was like. In a short time I knew his private history (which is of no interest here), his tastes in clothes, how much money a month he had at his disposal, and a variety of insignificant details that would have amazed you. He was an undeniably good-looking young boy, too perfect both in body and in face, as fair as you were dark, a weak boy, as most beautiful males are, clinging to you in admiration and in love, for the weakness of the stooge was merely an accentuation of that of every individual: he was even lonelier than most.

Pausing in the search for an adequate wife for you, I considered becoming friendly with the stooge, but that, I realized, was, in the end, merely postponing an eventual, certain fight.

When the stooge took up bachelor's quarters a few blocks

from your apartment I began to hurry in my wife-search. I overlooked no one, not even the girls who passed me in the street, who sat next to my table in restaurants and tearooms. I became extraordinarily friendly, talking to any young woman with whom I could strike up a conversation. Somewhere, I told myself, was the one I could use, somewhere.

I almost missed her when I found her, for at first glance I discarded her on the grounds that she was too similar to myself. Not until well into the meat course of a fashionable dinner-party, during which I listened to her voice at the other end of the table and at the same time gave polite answers to my host, did it occur to me that her very similarity to me was my safeguard, and I was impatient for coffee to be served in the drawing-room so that I could talk to her. I was excited at the prospect and I dubbed her, in my mind, the novia, using the warm Spanish word that means "bride." Even later, when I learned her name, I never thought of her except as the novia.

She was dark-haired and slender, as am I, although a full head taller; she held a part-time job on one of the local English-language newspapers; she had a mongrel parentage that gave her a certain exotic glamour; had been educated and had lived a long time in New York and, as a result, exuded that unmistakable New York aura of practicability mixed with a certain world-weary sentimentalism. She was doing well in her job, she told me, it was leading up to a fine offer on a big New York daily, with a by-line and a fat weekly check. Young men were not going to distract her from so luscious a career; they were good for lunches and as escorts for dances and to pay the bar bill. We chatted apart from the other guests, stirring third and then fourth cups of coffee, in a one-sided information-please. All the while, I thought elatedly that at last I had the stooge by the tail and, through him, you.

My campaign was carefully planned. It began with four dozen red roses which I sent her the following morning. This led to a telephone call which in turn led to a tea-date in town. That gave an opening for an invitation to the house for a swim, then for lunch, then for the weekend. I knew her a full month before I brought you to her; I had fattened her and melted her and she was ripe to meet you; I had made her curious with oblique references to you, by showing her a particularly good photo of you, by deferring to your judgment in arguments so that, by the time she met you, she was half in love with you already. As for you, I played the game both ways. I teased you with the prospect of her, I pointed out the newspaper articles or editorials or interviews she had written; once, meeting you by chance shopping in a department store immediately after leaving her, I pointed out to you her retreating back. You were avid to meet her; you pushed me, and the stooge, too, in the background in your sudden interest in this phenomenon that I had found. Because *I* had found her, you did not doubt that she *was* a phenomenon. You were worried that you might miss her, and you were insanely jealous that I had something you thought you wanted and that I was withholding it.

I arranged the meeting between you with seeming negligence and was prepared for all outcomes. The most logical result was inevitable, so well buttered you two were towards each other. You left the house together and I heard you propose a luncheon date for the following day. For a time I invited both of you together to the house, then I took to telling one to bring the other; by then you no longer mentioned the stooge and you were hopelessly and foolishly in love with the novia. Had you not been, after my painstaking work, I doubt that I could have realized my goal with you.

To be *in love* is in itself degrading, whereas *to love* is, by the same token, ennobling. *In love* is a game; in other languages it is perhaps more exactly expressed: in German, for example, where "verliebt" had a definitely depreciative connotation. You were in love with all the calfishness that I wished you to expend anywhere except on myself. This *in love* was like a weak liquid which you were draining off the better to come to me with the strong, heavy concentrate that had remained in you.

Absorbed in the novia, it never occurred to you that any other woman could override and consume your absorption, least of all myself, who had so magnanimously, so thoughtfully brought you this milk-and-honey in-loveness. You buzzed, an absurd beetle trying his wings, within the cage where I had confined you.

I began to advocate marriage between you and the novia, working first on the one and then on the other. I wished to be sure that, if your marriage would be a convenience to me, I would encounter no difficulties in putting it over.

During this ardent courtship of yours, the stooge was temporarily eliminated. You came with your novia to my house to listen to music, drink brandies on the terrace, give her swimming lessons in the pool, borrow books from me to lend to her, and, above all, show off to her what a magnificent, irreplaceable and unique friend you had. The stooge wasn't good enough to be dragged into the wooing; I remained the prize exhibit. My success had been brilliant and I relaxed, over the wrong issue. My vigilance over you and your novia never diminished, but I made the mistake of underestimating the resiliency of the stooge. It is always difficult for those who are surfeited to realize the hunger of the desperate, and the stooge had been too happy with the blossoming friendship to relinquish it altogether. He waited, quiet, forgotten, faithful and miserable in a twilight background of infinite patience.

In my effort to consume you, instead of allowing you to consume me, I assigned to you a certain definite part in my life and I could not afford that you trespass beyond the boundaries I determined. This definite part of my life had then to be an extraordinary one because it must compensate for not being the whole. Of course the whole embraced it, but without it the whole would be valueless. The pit in the peach is a small part of the fruit compared with the flesh and skin that surrounds it, yet the flesh and skin could not exist were it not for the pit, and the pit is the being of the peach.

As the pit with the peach, so her sex with a woman. It frequently happens that, in the act of loving and being loved by a man, a woman is bruised, is hurt, and the hurt itself is so delicious, so exquisitely satisfying that she demands its repetition, its prolongation. The hurt becomes the essence and

77

the meaning of what she is doing. You yourself, your presence, your being in the world at all, was exactly identical to this hurt. You were the reason for my pleasure and my pleasure was a perpetual, sharp and unending pain provoked exclusively because of and by you.

I do not doubt that it was the same with you.

At no time was I ever eclipsed by your noisy furore over your novia; you were doping and deluding and deadening yourself to forget the tormenting pain of me.

Knowing this, the violent need to touch you, to stroke you, to be assured by the most banal of physical contacts with you, diminished. I held you always within me, what use to repeat the inner action by gross outward manifestations? The time would come when there would need to be between us something different from the usual pettings and kisses and penetrations. These emotional weeds were for your novia. Whatever that something was, I did not know; I guessed, lazily, unhurriedly.

How, then, did we first approach each other in the construction of our relationship of love? A combination of circumstances led to it, an increase of presents from you to me (everything you saw you wanted to buy for me) and a temporary cooling-off of your novia towards you plus her open questioning of the altruism of my interest in you, a matter where you galloped to my defence.

There was a holiday at that time and your novia, in an ill-timed squabble with you, arranged to leave town for an all-day picnic with another admirer rapidly shoved into the role of rival. You complained to me, and I shrugged the affair away, claiming it had no importance exactly because I saw that it had, for me, all the importance in the world. It deposited you, unsuspecting and innocent, in my lap. I asked you if you would like to spend the afternoon with me and you assented quickly.

"All right, then," I told you. "But come after lunch. I have guests."

You wondered at the time why I did not invite you with the others; how could you guess I was arranging a span of hours with you alone and unmolested?

It was a lovely, sunny, spring-like afternoon, when the orange trees flowered and the air was heavy with their rich scent. The river breeze soothed as it ruffled through our clothes, the sun mellowed us without unduly warming us, nature displayed herself in her most deceiving friendliness.

We mounted bicycles and pedalled about the sleepy suburbs and along the paths that followed the flat expanse of river; I watched you do improbable and unnecessary things with the wheel which little boys of twelve perform for their sweethearts of the sixth grade. You were constantly shouting at me: "Mamma, mamma, watch me stand on my head!" I wondered why men, when they are happy, invariably revert to little boys but women, once adult, never become little girls again unless it be for the express purpose of seducing some adolescent male with baby-talk and the like. This little boy in men I found peculiarly irritating. Of the many attributes which I had valued in my dead husband (and where you suffered grievously by comparison) his never reverting to little-boyness was certainly an important one. You almost

79

ran into a car, entirely by your own doing, twice you fell from the bicycle, you insisted upon scooting ahead of me to take the lead without knowing where we were going, you braked and speeded; by the time we returned to the house for tea I was heartily sick of this pubescent cavorting.

To my relief, you became adult after tea and by dinner you were in full stride as a man. After coffee we played records on the gramophone in the music-room, producing quartets and trios at will. I allowed you to select the records; "our" music did not exist between us despite all the concert hours we had spent together so you were obliged to create an atmosphere for yourself, a mood; my function would be to select the moment for action within that mood. Mine were everlastingly, in our relationship, the daring acts.

You, too, knew that ahead was the moment when you would commit yourself to me and postponed reaching it by every device you could summon to assist you. By the time it was expedient to take leave of me you decided on "one last record" and chose (having considered this selection for the past two hours) a disc we had played several times already on significant if innocent occasions, an Easter record; you were looking for "our" music. As a Bach lover (even to this point the university intruded) you wanted the suitable tones for the moment. We fenced with quick words and side looks and smiles. The moment was being so finely protracted that it was becoming unbearable; it was an exquisite prototype of sexual climax executed by every sense save tactile. The windows were open and the orange-blossom air swirled in the room, its heaviness could be tasted, the music sang out clear and pure, the muted lamplight showed us to each other as shadows. Standing beside you, I lifted your left hand—for you are left-handed—and, opening the palm, kissed it in the immemorial gesture of women to the men they accept as lovers. What could you do except reach for my hand too? That was the moment you betrayed the novia and committed yourself to me forever.

I do not know if it is considered a superstition to believe in omens; in any case, I do. For example, one goes shopping in the morning and everything seems wrong, there are no salesgirls able to attend one, the store is crowded, the article one seeks is out of stock; or, one is balked in a business deal, the partners will not sign the contract, the lawyer is delayed in his arrival, the board of directors lacks a quorum. What additional signals does one require to realize the day is not auspicious for shopping or for business and that it is wiser to become an inconspicuous nonentity until the jinx has passed. There are lesser omens, too; when we utilize an incident in order to obtain a result (as, later, I was to find out you thought, too). One says to oneself: "If I win this set of tennis that means that tonight Betty—or Jane or Susy—will kiss me." Or, "If I walk on the curb rim for a block without falling off, I'll get a salary raise." There is no logic to any of this but it becomes vital to win the tennis set and walk on the curb rim, and if, by lucky coincidence, Betty kisses or the boss raises the salary one becomes an involuntary convert to such idiocies and we are each of us, however, protestingly, just such converts.

Where you kissed me, on the palm of my right hand, a

strange rash broke out during the night and in the morning I caught my hand on the satin of my comforter. I examined this rash closely, studying it: it was as if a four-pronged fork had scraped across the skin leaving in its wake harsh, hard scrub-ends of dead tissue protruding colorlessly to ruin silk stockings and scratch against delicate dress fabrics and expensive bedspreads. I contemplated this unexpected eruption in my hand for a long time, sitting in the sun before my dressing-table. It was neither red nor livid, as new hurts should be; it was dry and mature. I took it as an omen.

"So long as it lasts," I told myself, "my present relationship with him will continue. When it goes, it signifies a transition."

I never showed the mark to you, nor mentioned it.

With that seemingly pious but actually very wicked kiss in the palm of my hand came a renascence of the gaudy thrills and excitements that I had already experienced in the university years ago, only this time how much more meaningful, how much more dangerous. In the university, it had been beauty itself which I had loved, much in the way of Aschenbach's feelings to Tadzio in Mann's *Death in Venice*. That what was beauty to me was no beauty at all to others did not matter. I used to wait for the girl to cross the campus, to pass near me at lunch hour when we filed into the dining-room, to sit beside me in the library doubled over some heavy book, to be visible anywhere so that I might admire, desire and agitate. It seemed so much of an effort to lay aside my worshipping appreciation and get to work to make friends with her. I loved my own passion, I was delighted I could feel so violently; I worried only that perhaps the violence could be intensified, and if I did not reach its limits I would miss something wonderful and unique. I dared never test my own emotion, nor did she, for I lacked confidence and wisdom and this whole teapot-passion never reached a proper climax. I was inordinately pleased with myself at the time for having the talent to create anything so beautiful and to convince myself, with the aid of an awakening erotic interest, of its validity. I loved, as most of us do in excessive youth, blindly, seeing nothing of reality and believing implicitly in the creation of my imagination. Had such beauty as I was loving actually existed, the whole campus of twelve hundred girls would have been in a ferment of Lesbian revolt.

In loving you, I had travelled the long road between loving blindly and loving with the most awful of acute perceptions. I should have been relieved for the respite of blindness in my love for you.

Any but physical feeling is created by imagination. Every grade and degree of loving is only so much imagination, working at varying speeds; it is self-created. In the same way that we have called into being, either through hysteria or sickness or deliberate want, a so-called "feeling," we are able to destroy it. *I love* or *I hate* is the perfect example of the activity of our imaginative powers. The grande passion—immortalized by literature if seldom in the flesh—comes to those with the greatest imaginative facility. Loving and hating takes place *in our own minds;* our bodies, as a consequence of the mental state we have entered (with what hard work, lies and treacheries!) produce ample evidence of our emotion.

Thinking itself, as Hegel has said, is merely a process of separating one thing from another. Love is at once a ludicrous and proud example of just this separation; we separate *one* individual from *all* others, concentrate on him and arouse in ourselves a self-willed interest in and affection for him. With assiduous cultivation (in which we are amply aided by family and friends if we are virgins, and by advertisements, movies and the classics if we aren't) this becomes coincident with a strong and agreeable sexual desire, and then we are prone to say we "love." To be truthful, we ought to say: "Hurray! I've managed to get myself in that frame of mind where I think I love." This would be too unromantic; better to conceive of love (and sell it in different forms) as something that has to do with moonlight and roses and scented letters and certain recognizable expressions of the eyes and identifiable touches of the hands. That love should be nothing more than a mental conception is understandably irritating; love, to be tabulated and palatable, to insure marriage and, with vigilance, monogamy also, must be distinguishable from all other possible emotions; it must concur with the "good" (that is, the morals, however foolish, of society), it must be striven for in a kind of medieval way. As a result, an incredible amount of propaganda is turned out about it, everything from Sappho's poetry to the latest Cole Porter.

*"The moon has set, and the Pleiads; it is the middle of the night
and time passes, time passes, and I lie alone,"*

is merely a more universal and moving way of saying,
"So near and yet so far from me."

Ask anybody, the next person one sees, for example, *what
is love?* and he will stammer and stutter an involved definition that totals *sex.* Ask, indeed, twenty people and no two
will agree save that the proper expression of loving is best
demonstrated in bed. Substituting *desire,* or even *copulation*
for *love,* the same conclusion is reached. What is love?
What is sex? Is sex love? Is love sex? Can desire be love? Is
love still love when infected by admitted carnality? The
questions, and the variations on the themes thereof, are unending. Custom, mores, education, taboos, the poems we've
read, the songs we know, the forbidden books snitched from
the parental library will determine our answer and, of
course, this answer will have nothing whatsoever to do with
the truth.

You defined love as "having contact with somebody who
will enable one to fulfill oneself." A more practical definition, a more usable philosophy of love would be difficult to
find. If nothing else, I admired, when you gave me this definition, your boundless, limitless egotism.

*"Love . . . like insanity . . . sees everything; it must not re-
veal its thought."*—Christina Stead.
"Love is an abject intercourse between tryants and slaves."—
Oliver Goldsmith.
"Love is the coldest of critics."—George M. Curtis.

85

"Love is a spirit all compact of fire."—Shakespeare.
"Love is the sweetest thing on earth."—J. J. Roche.
"Love is a sickness full of woes."—Sam Daniel.

Such a variety of definitions on the most talked-of subject in the world makes one conclude that no two people have the same idea as to what love actually is. The consensus is that it is like something else, preferably a part of nature; are we then any the wiser? Some of the definitions are contradictory, flat denials of others. How can we help realizing we have no more idea of what love is than we have a knowledge of the elusive germ that brings on a cold in the nose?

One drizzly, sad afternoon I visited your apartment. I was relieved to desert the wetness of the streets for the dry comfort of your bachelor's flat. I had had to walk from the station uphill, through the light, clammy rain, for there were no taxis.

You opened the door promptly to my ring; I congratulated myself on having arrived unobserved and, once the strain of obtaining your apartment was over, I looked about me from force of habit, struck each time with the charmless aspect of your quarters.

Impersonally was, without doubt, the proper adjective to convey a succinct description of how you lived. It was obvious you lacked the courage to assert your personality by indulging in a bold color-scheme, original materials or out-of-the-ordinary furniture. Had I not already discovered how timid you were I would have known through this. With two exceptions, every item in your flat was hopelessly conventional, unobtrusive and boring. A decorator, endeavoring to recall the furnishings, would have had difficulty; there was nothing outstanding to fasten on; the place was as anonymous as a second-rate hotel suite. The two exceptions were a Bolivian primitive painting hanging against the patterned wall, totally at variance with the unimaginative décor of the room, and a small, very perfect Ming vase that stood on a black, carved lacquer foot in its own specially made partition of one of the bookshelves. The Ming vase demanded a warm and elegant room in which its mature simplicity could be displayed properly; the Bolivian primitive looked as out of place as a gorgeous native costume would look in a New York broker's office.

I wandered about the living-room restlessly, reading the titles of your books, standing before the wide window to view the grey river in the distance through a haze of rain. Turning to face the room again, I noticed with a mechanical, housewifely eye that everything was scrupulously neat and clean; there was not even the romance of dirt.

Standing in the living-room near your desk, I commented, as I had so often before, that the Bolivian primitive wasn't so bad, and you told me the involved story I already knew by heart of how you had stumbled on it in a small mountain village, paying some ancient Indian a few pesos for it. I crossed to the bookshelves and lifted the Ming vase from its wooden foot and held it in my hands, turning it around to admire its form, its pattern; it felt cool in my fingers. Although I had held it many times before you had never vouchsafed any information about it and I had never asked. Now you suddenly volunteered:

"That's my good-luck piece."

That you, too, were superstitious was a revelation to me, but then why shouldn't you have your pet foible, which is, in the last analysis, merely some outmoded voodoo brought up-to-date. Despite our modern scientific educations we are all still prone to invest certain inanimate objects with qualities they obviously cannot possess. I understood that the Ming vase, if not precisely an absolute "good-luck" piece, certainly had a specific importance for you.

"It's pretty," I admired, now that you had lifted it out of the limbo of tabu. "Where did you get it?"

"It was given to me," you answered, almost sullenly, no doubt regretting having admitted me into this intimate chamber of your past.

I needed, then, little imagination to know who had given it to you and why, although names and dates were, of course, beyond my guessing. This Ming vase, I reconstructed, was a gift to you from your first mistress. It represented your initial success as a man, if not your initial experience. I could surmise this mistress had been a married woman of taste, that the affair had been conducted on a romantic, tragic level and that the little vase remained the symbol of uninhibited passion at its best; wild, uncalculating passion as we are allowed to know it—and be burned by it—just once in our youth. I replaced the Ming vase carefully on its lacquered pedestal.

I came and stood beside you at the window, without touching you, and we both watched the rain and the changing slate hues on the distant river.

"Do you like poetry?" I asked you carelessly, for it struck me as an afternoon made for poetic people, the kind of texture and color of day that would have delighted Verlaine or de Musset.

"No," you denied brusquely.

"Afraid of it?" I pressed, slyly.

"Certainly not!" you defended yourself. "Although it's rather more a subject for women than for men."

"Still, most poetry is written by men," I pointed out.

"I can't quite imagine a female Shakespeare or Dante or Heine. Can you?" You still faced the river; morosely you stared at the rooftops shining in the rain.

In a rush, stringing all the words together, I flung the anonymous fifteenth-century jingle at you. I chanted in a monotone:

> *"Western wind, when wilt thou blow*
> *That the small rain down can rain?*
> *Christ, that my love were in my arms*
> *And I in my bed again!"*

I saw you repeating the words to yourself, your lips moving silently and, as you realized the rhyme, you turned to me and asked uncertainly:

"Is that poetry? It's nice."

"Everything that has to do with love is nice," I reminded you.

"Everything that has to do with you is nice," you replied, looking at me steadily.

"Oh, nice, not nice," I exploded impatiently. "Actually, love isn't at all nice. It's exciting or terrifying, but nice? It's much too cutting to be nice!"

You put a hand on my head and ran your fingers down my hair, not touching my cheek at all, and half-smiled at me.

"What an odd word you used," you commented. "Cutting."

"It's not my choice," I admitted, anxious to give justice where justice was due, especially if that wouldn't harm me.

"I know," you nodded, pulling at the strands of my hair. "It's Baudelaire's."

"But I thought," I began in surprise, and then stopped for of course you had not actually said you were ignorant of poetry; you merely had led me to believe that you had the usual schoolboy's lack of knowledge of it.

"Poets have their uses," you said. "They make things sound more important than they are," and you dropped your hand from my hair. "Now and then they clarify our own thoughts, or express our desires more succinctly. What would love be without language?"

Privately, I thought it wouldn't exist, except as love can be said to exist for the mare and the stallion.

"Nobody doubts the power of words," I granted.

"But there's still something more powerful," you inserted quickly before I could continue. "Although, naturally, it can't reach as many people as words do, what with amplifiers and radios."

"Something more powerful than words?" I repeated, frowning. "And what is that?"

"Touch," you replied shortly, and grazed your fingertips over my face.

CHAPTER SIX

One evening you offered to take me to dinner and to a concert in the penthouse of some musical friends. We had neither dinner nor concert, for when you called for me you drove not to a restaurant but to your own apartment where we became so absorbed in talking that both dinner and concert were forgotten.

You had something on your mind, something in particular you wished to discuss and, remembering your remark "one final escape" which you had let slip in one of my

visits to your flat, I was anxious to hear what you might
have to say. I dared not hope you would, already in our relationship, show me the road I must follow where you were
concerned.

"Have you ever thought of killing yourself?" you asked
me abruptly, whirling around in your pacing up and down
the room to watch my face.

"No."

"Oh, of course," you observed tartly, "you have known
only the good life and lived off the fat of the land."

"That's not true," I contradicted calmly.

"Then why haven't you thought of killing yourself? I
have." You spoke violently, aggressively, as if accusing me
of an omission of good conduct.

"I suppose I love life too much and, added to that, I'm
afraid to die," I answered slowly. "I'm so afraid to die, you
see, that I'm forever thanking God, or Nature, or Destiny,
whatever you care to call it, for having permitted me to enjoy the day I have just lived through."

"But don't circumstances ever become so complicated for
you that it's simply too much trouble to unravel them?"

"No," I told you shortly.

"You never get tired of the endless scandal and misunderstandings and trickeries and scenes and quarrels?"

"I enjoy them," I confessed candidly.

"But when things start to repeat," you objected, "doesn't
it seem too much of an effort to go through it all again?"

"Nothing ever repeats."

"Everything is repetition!" you claimed hotly, and wheeled

93

from me, your hands shoved deep in your trousers pockets. You went to examine the Ming vase. Your preoccupation and insistence upon the repetitiousness of events impressed me as being a sort of inexplicable and unhealthy obsession, as if you were afraid to meet anything new and unknown.

I called to you across the room and asked you to come and sit beside me on the sofa. You obeyed slowly; I noticed as you came nearer that your eyes had become cloudy. When you were settled opposite me I leaned over you and kissed your lips, without hurry and without timidity. I felt your tongue boldly exploring my mouth. Drawing away from you I smiled and asked:

"Is this repetition?"

You slid your hands slowly downward from my hair and let them come to rest on my shoulders.

"Yes and no," you answered. *"Yes,* because I've known all along the end implicit in the beginning of our relationship, and *no,* because there is the possibility you might change the end, although I doubt you can. I'm merely speculating on an unlikelihood."

I considered your answer; the "yes and no" disturbed me and I stored it in my mind for future examination.

"And because one knows the climax implicit in a kiss," I countered, "is that a reason to forgo the kiss?"

"Is there reason to kissing?" you demanded, and drew me over you, to embrace me more detailedly.

"It is like snowflakes," I said after a time, lying relaxed in your arms.

"What is?" you asked drowsily.

"Kissing," I said meditatively, "or anything else pleasant that one does repetitiously, like shopping or taking a bath. All snowflakes are made of the same thing, frozen water, just as a kiss is made of air, but no two snowflakes ever have the same pattern, nature is inexhaustibly diverse. In the same way no mouth can repeat its kiss. It is perhaps not a very clear comparison," I apologized, "snowflakes and kisses, but it's the best I can do. If you say each snowflake is a repetition, a duplication of every other snowflake, that isn't strictly true. Each snowflake is recognizable as a snowflake, but not identical. The same with kisses."

"It is not so much the kissing that troubles me," you said, "but the necessary phraseology that goes with it, the eternal mumbling of the same few words, the poverty of expression. On every other subject it's possible to be so voluble. But not on this."

"So now that their meaning finally coincides with their text," I finished for you, "you will refuse to say them?"

"I refuse to say them," you repeated, "no matter if they are utterly and purely true. They've been tainted and distorted like everything that becomes public property. If you need them, go read any cheap backstairs novel; you'll find them fifty times in as many pages. *I love you, Percival,*'" you mimicked in a highpitched falsetto, "*'And I love you,' the handsome man told little orphan Annie,*" you went on in a deep bass. "I hate the words! Everybody says them to everybody. They're a nightmare. I love you, I love chocolate ice-cream, I'd love to come to dinner. Has ever a word been so abused? Don't talk, don't talk," you ordered, holding my

95

head on your shoulder and putting a hand over my mouth, shoving your fingers against my teeth.

Returned home, I sat in the library, smoking a cigarette, and watched the blue smoke spiral entertainingly before my eyes. What was it, I asked myself, that I wanted of you?

Women, I knew, do not care about men, unsupportable as this may be to the male vanity; women care about *things*. Their desires are always specific, they want the darling red-and-green dress in the window of the most expensive shop in town, or the seat at the ambassador's right at an embassy dinner, or the momentarily attractive physique of the blond Adonis in the drug-store. To secure these ends, women have developed an intricate and successful system of scheming and plotting which has nothing whatsoever to do with thinking. Woman never loses her battle, for, being entirely material-istic, she has only to pursue her desire long enough and as-tutely enough and then she must inevitably obtain it. Entirely grabby, woman is by instinct and talent on the winning side.

Men, slower and stupider, by virtue of being slower discover causes to embrace, ideals to live up to, principles to follow, and by virtue of stupidity fight an obstinate battle even when they might lose. The satisfaction a woman derives from possessing a thing is equalled by the man possessing an *idea* of the thing; the idea of a textile industry to manufacture the darling red-and-green dresses, the idea of being honored by an important personage, the idea of love.

Men produce and create ideas and their womenfolk use these ideas. There are always bisexual oddities through history, such as Shakespeare and Michelangelo, Sappho and Emily Brontë, who can combine the function of creating the idea and at the same time of using it. These rarities are inimitable; one must be born to oddity, impossible to fake it.

What, if anything, could I, woman, want of you, man?

I had been sated long before meeting you with darling red-and-green dresses; dull dinner chatter with foolish ambassadors are too boring to be worth the chair at their right; too many dresses, jewels and perfumes become a bother what with cleaners' bills, insurance and evaporation. Women, materially and socially satisfied, begin—like well-fed, sleek jungle beasts—to look about for something exciting to do; some become historical figures, a Medici, a Borgia, a Messalina; most, operating in a quiet way, are never heard of, although the results of their work—or play—may be startlingly evident.

What had you, or any man, to give me that I might want, that might be useful to me, or instructive, or pleasurable?

Usually, when women turn to men, it is in the happy delusion that the man they have selected will "understand" them, "love" them, "provide for" them, "make a good father," and, in general, nurse them through the whole complicated process of living. If they turn from one man, their husband, let us say, to another, their lover, it is in the assumption that the lover will be more satisfactory than the husband, and the period during which they discover, bit by bit, that the lover is as selfish, thoughtless, incompetent, careless and ineffective as the husband is referred to as the love affair. Sometimes, since neither man nor woman is by nature

97

monogamous regardless of how much pressure is put upon us by Church and Society to be so, sometimes a sexual change of scenery satisfies the discontented woman and she returns to her husband after a brief carnal flurry or flirtation; after all, the husband isn't quite so wearying. In the end, it is difficult for human beings to love and easy for them to fornicate; but how unflattering to the ego to admit this; far better to be sophisticated and say "sex is love" and let it go at that, or, to be utterly specific, voluntary carnality is love, the rest comes under the heading of prostitution or gigolo-ism.

In my relationship with you I had deliberately omitted what has always seemed to me a particularly offensive phase in the coming together of a man and woman, namely, I had not obliged you, by a series of well-worked-out coynesses on my part, to chase me with the familiar tribal primitivity. Theoretically, a man places no value on a woman he can have without conquering, and by *have* I mean possess physically. Since I was not primarily interested in sleeping with you, being neither virgin nor abused, I saw no necessity for the ludicrous sexual chase. I never made myself inaccessible and I played no hide-and-seek with you. Since I was always reachable, always there, you came to look upon me as a part of your life, as much yours as your nose and hands; exactly as you could still live with your nose cut off, so could you live without me; it was possible but by no means pleasant. It would be difficult to devise a more adequate way to make sure of the fidelity—and here I do *not* mean the monogamy —of a man. Wherever you went, you thought of me, not necessarily with desire or lust, the variations of human relationships permit a host of other ways of being conscious of each other. You wanted me to read what you read, see what you saw, hear the music you heard; you wanted to discuss the news with me, or a business problem; you wanted to buy me a handbag or a pair of gloves; two blocks or twenty miles away from me you reacted the same to me. I was present in the back of your mind; your novia took care of the immediate front, you poured your desire over her and wondered what *I* might be like as your wife, even as you asked *her* to marry you.

It was impossible for me to postpone forever the day when I must decide to take action about you. This was as difficult and far-reaching in consequences as is the decision of a man to leave his home and make his life abroad, or to fix upon one career in preference to another. Did I want you as a husband, as a daily companion, as the creature for whom one cooks and cleans? Indeed I did, but not because I loved you with the domestic passion of the housewife but because I wanted to demonstrate to you what an admirable marvel I am as a wife, a home-maker, a playmate. My vanity wanted praise from you. That you already knew, and admitted; my talents in this direction were not sop enough for my greed; I wanted to prove *to* you, not have you witness the proof. I wanted the shrewish pleasure of licking my chops and saying to you, "You see how much better than you I can do everything!" I wanted, in brief, my vanity spoiled and soothed by you.

Did I want you as a friend? In no way, for friendship is

to my mind a polite hypocrisy. Once in a talk with you about the stooge you explained to me the quality of your friendship with him, extolling your mutual loyalty, the give-and-take between you, the reliability of both of you where the other was concerned. You became bright-eyed with the virtues of this friendship; there was nothing ulterior about it; it was all beautiful and clean. You spoke so much and so fluently that I was unable to insert even a word, and in despair, to stop the eulogistic flow of rhetoric, I wrote down on the reverse of the menu the apt definition of friendship by the Duc de la Rouchefoucauld and handed it to you across the luncheon table:

"Friendship . . . is a species of commerce out of which self-love always expects to gain something."

I was "friends with" so many people that I hardly needed you as one more to gratify further my sharp bargaining instincts.

Did I want you as a lover? Certainly yes, but I could not stomach the Technicolor movie my imagination reeled off for me of you and me clandestinely meeting for a hurried embrace, or of girlish raptures over your treasured, beribboned, entirely unoriginal love-letters, or of sentimental exchanges of handkerchiefs and locks of hair. Doesn't every woman want every man as her lover as a proof to herself of her own attractiveness?

Furthermore, "wanting" you as a lover was an impossibility. As soon as we began to know each other, and that was the first day we met, we were committed as lovers. Although

you often protested I wasn't "handling" you properly or that
I failed to understand you—which merely meant I refused to
indulge you in your undisciplined moods—you yourself offered these protests half-heartedly without the slightest hope
of their convincing either of us. Whether I wanted to or not,
I either understood you immediately or, if you puzzled me,
on reflection. Probably a good deal of what I loved in you
was merely a reflection of myself. There was also the element of flattery; I was pleased you found me irresistible,
that was a corroboration of my own good taste; and, no
doubt, some of it was erotic. If I didn't yearn for you, I still
enjoyed your embraces. I could hardly want what was not
withheld.

Were I to live with you, or any man who made a minimum living wage, how would my life differ from the life I
was leading? Probably I would borrow books to read instead
of buying private expensive editions, wear copies of models
instead of the originals, and buy a dime's worth of flowering
cactus instead of a fortune of hot-house chrysanthemums; I
should live in one room instead of in twenty, hang bargain-
counter curtains over the windows instead of hand-embroi-
dered imported voile, and paint junk-store furniture instead
of buying antiques. But would the *pattern* of my life be
changed, would I develop different tastes, new habits?
Hardly, for with the diminishing of comfort there comes an
increase of ingenuity; cunningly, I would obtain the things
I have always had but with a lower cash payment. The millionaire and the twelve-dollar-a-week man can still read the
same newspaper and window-shop on the same avenue and

even, if it is necessary to carry the analogy to the last heart throb, pick up the same stray dog and make a household pet of it.

Had you any importance to me and, if so, in what way?

Obviously, by my own interest in you, I gave you a certain importance in my life. Why did I do this? Probably I could not resist the male edition of myself, which you represented; partly I enjoyed the power—both of influence and seduction—which I, an older woman, could wield over you, a young man; and partly because I recognized you for the alluring quicksand you were, feeding on others and swallowing up any personality bold enough to come too close to you. In conclusion, to prove you a weaker person than myself, I was obliged—in order to sustain my own self-confidence—to vanquish you. *I* had not made this into a death-struggle: *we* had.

What did you want of me?

You were satisfied with my choice of wife for you; you relied on my judgment to pick the best, why should you seek further? When you claimed you wanted me as a friend you yourself laughed and held me against you in a way that left friendship limping far behind. As your mistress I troubled your conscience too much, you were neither wealthy nor experienced enough to digest a mistress and your work, your health and purse and your personal relationships suffered. Yet, you wanted me to love you, and if I refused to cherish you above myself, you took second place greedily and hoped for and dreamed of first. You wanted me to die for you as a sign of your own worth.

We realized and resented in varying intensities our need of each other. I was, for you, the most delightful and informed teacher you could ever hope to find, and for me you were that spark—even that fire—that maintained my youthfulness alive within me. We were, furthermore, each other's guinea-pigs, for we experimented everlastingly on one another. We lived, within ourselves, like maelstroms, and we sought a proper expression and control of our energies for our own comfort. We both admitted, half-laughingly, that we looked forward to the peace-by-exhaustion of old age; since I doubted I should live that long that was an additional, justifying reason for me to fulfill my plan towards you. Why should you have anything I could not have?

One day, walking from your apartment to the local suburban station through a small, hilly park studded with flowerbeds and with the heavy, contorted branches of a large jacaranda glorying in its center, you asked me, abruptly, what part of the Bible I liked best.

"The Psalms," I answered reflectively, "and the Song of Solomon and the Jacob-and-Joseph. Why do you ask?"

You shook your head at me and drew me to a seat on one of the gay green park benches. At this hour of the warm afternoon the park was deserted, the children were home taking their naps and the workers were still at their jobs. In the whole city I doubt that anybody would have thought to look for us on a park bench.

"That's not what I mean," you said earnestly. "When somebody says to you *The Bible,* what do you think of?

Sunday-school, God, religion, a black book with small type? What?"

"I think of a phrase, as a matter of fact," I confessed.

"So do I," you said quickly. "Did you think of it today in the apartment when we were together?"

"Yes." I looked at you curiously. Was it just barely possible, I wondered, that we thought of the same phrase? "Did you?" I prodded.

You nodded and told me to quote mine.

Sitting there in the shade of the jacaranda, a strange thing happened to me which at the time I did not in the least understand but which later became apparent to me. It seemed to me that there was again a *humming* between us as when I had first met you, only much louder, as if we were both singing the same song in the same key, a perfect attunement between us, actually soundless, but very clear in my head. I knew then, for a certainty, that we had each picked, out of the thousands of wonderful, rich Biblical phrases, the same phrase; it was the only one thoroughly applicable to us. To restless people such as we there is always only one boon, one gift which we cannot give ourselves naturally no matter how much wealth or power we have. I remember looking around the park at the tall lilac-blue agapantos, watching the sprinklers revolve shoots of water, and thinking irrelevantly how somnolent all this was. Without effort, even without thought, I gave you my phrase.

"He giveth his beloved sleep," I said, so low that you bent towards me to hear.

You looked at me triumphantly as if to say, "I've won because I knew it, I've won!" and then your expression soured and you said bitterly:

"Yes, and of what use sleep if you dream? Or don't you dream?"

Then I knew that in your sleep, as in mine, there was still no respite from each other. I was, at this time, so absorbed with you that I dreamt of you nightly; no strange, illogical, Freudian dreams but quite the contrary. I spoke to you as a rule in my own language, very occasionally in yours, and we had long dialogues about our plans, our wants, our likes and dislikes, our ideas, and sometimes, awakening in the morning, I honestly did not know how much had been dream and how much had already taken place in physical actuality.

In the dreams you were as natural as in reality, down to the smallest detail. Sometimes my dreams were rehearsals of meetings I planned to have with you, more often they were repetitions, with only minor distortions, of what had already taken place between us. I learned, gradually, to utilize my dreams, and I was able, with some concentration and the patient persistence of trying, each night, to make you do, in my dreams, what I wished you to do. In my dreams, I had great freedom of action and the most I demanded of you was submission. Very likely, every capable woman sees herself, in dreams or day-dreams, as a lover instead of the everlastingly passive, acquiescent beloved. Even the mildest and most inhibited of us have our unconfessed moments when we want to attack. So I unclothed you, caressed you, slept with you, examined you, talked to you, talked endlessly, unceasingly to you. I laid the scene for these dreams in your apartment as I felt it was less of an effort than to create an entirely new background. I read, in my dreams, the letters in your desk, I looked over the suits hanging in your closet, rifling their pockets, I opened the drawers of your bureau, I flipped the leaves of your books and studied the photographs in your albums. It would be an exaggeration to say that everything I did in my dreams proved to be, upon investigation of the reality, correct. Upon awakening, I could not remember the contents of the letters or books, or of the closet and bureau drawers but I could recall, as I found out by analysing my dreams, anything that I had already seen; that is, the title of a book you had loaned me from your collection or that had impressed me when looking over your bookshelves, the name of the woman who had written the letter if you had mentioned her to me, the suits or ties I had seen you wear, the photos you had shown me. I spent six or seven hours with you every night in the greatest intimacy.

Inevitably, we squirmed, rationalized, ran away, sought substitutions or even ignored in an effort to escape each other; this was so much useless gymnastics; we were condemned to each other because we had taken each other seriously, we were mutually important (were we not important to ourselves?). We were unable to relinquish each other, having become viruses in each other's blood, flowing evenly through the bloodstream, warm, palpitating and as permanent as our lives. To marry would have been misery; one cannot marry oneself, one marries to get away from oneself. Living was difficult enough without having the martyrdom of living with two of ourselves, seeing unremittingly our double in the other sex. All of us think, at some point in our lives, *what would I have been like had I been born a man (or a woman) instead?* As speculation, this is pleasant, diverting; as reality, it is an impossibility and intolerable.

To resume: had I married you, I would have strangled the possibility of any further development of myself as a person; I would have annihilated myself, for whatever you *could* be to me, you *could not* be my teacher. When the teacher sells out to the pupil, or the stronger to the weaker or even the good to the evil, it signifies a slavery that can result only in the demolition of the character, intelligence and personality of the lunatic individual who has deliberately handed over the structure of his life for wreckage by the enemy. Whatever crimes I might need to commit, whatever voids I should have to conquer, whatever horrors I should need to surmount, the preservation of *my* integrity justified everything. *My* goal, the maintaining of myself complete, tolerated, even approved, *any* means.

It seemed unreal and melodramatic to tell myself as I watched you play tennis or place records on the gramophone or serve yourself a whisky-and-soda, that I must eliminate you, be rid of you for my own welfare, shunt you out of the world, for there was insufficient space for us in the immensity of this world to endure each other; because wherever you were, I must come, because we would torment, obsess, analyse and fight each other until our strength were drained and sickness or insanity overtook us. Had I been so beneficial to you that my merely being alive was a stimulus to you the problem would not have existed, but the better you knew me the worse your work became, the fewer your personal relationships, the heavier the books you read, the gloomier the music you wanted to hear and the more extravagant your moods became. Were you beneficial to me? Not at all, for, with you alive, I lived in suspension, as it were, waiting for the moment when either I would eradicate you and free myself of the thought of being with you, or actually be with you for the few hours that invariably corroborated my necessity to destroy you.

I determined to be finished with you, choosing a special time to begin this destruction. The decision taken, I tried to live with it, to make it a natural part of me, to take the odious idea of death to my bosom and so be at peace when the time came to execute it.

CHAPTER SEVEN

The episode
of the tennis-match gave me a good indication to what extent I still controlled myself and the situation between us. The actual basis of the episode was insignificant. A shortage of petrol swept over the town and transportation by private car became difficult; cruising taxis disappeared from the city streets, Sunday drivers vanished and large cars were left in the garages as being too voracious consumers of the precious gasoline. Coupons were distributed and lucky people with

chauffeurs, like myself, or with office-boys at their call, like you, could send chauffeur and boy to wait in line at the gasoline pumps for hours on end; the unlucky car-owning multitudes fumed and fretted a whole day away waiting for their turn at the pump. So long as chauffeur and office-boy were available, this gas-by-proxy system worked admirably, but one weekend the chauffeur fell ill, and I was stranded with an empty tank. It was the weekend of the national tennis championship, the only weekend I could be counted upon to leave the comfort of home to sit on a hot, stony bench in a broiling sun for the pleasure of watching two heavily sweating contestants play their hearts out in the unbearable heat for the privilege to be acquired by one of them of hugging a silver cup, half his height, to his bosom. The finals were scheduled for Sunday and we discussed it, you and I, on the preceding day, talking over the chances of each contestant; I complained about the difficulties of transportation.

"Oh, but I'll be glad to take you in my car and bring you back," you offered. "Sunday trains are impossible, and I doubt there are any taxis to be had." You explained you had planned to go for weeks, taking your novia with you, but you hadn't got around to buying the tickets yet. We arranged to go together after a swim and luncheon at the house, as the weather was so warm and sticky it was only fair to offer you and your novia a cooling dip before the hot afternoon.

Sunday was cruelly hot and we dawdled in the pool as long as we could; you and your novia splashed and shouted like healthy puppies; the drive in your car to the championship courts was, by contrast, doubly oppressive.

As all events, even the slightest, have their forewarning, so had this one.

The contestants for the finals were popular and, as a result, for hundreds of yards to either side of the entrance to the tennis club, there was a long row of parked cars. Everybody who had petrol, it seemed, had come to the matches. You hung out of the window of the car, cruising slowly, looking for a possible empty space into which you could squeeze, something near the entrance of the club.

On the opposite side of the road you found what you wanted and swung the car around to back into it, completely ignoring a smaller car that was already trying to occupy the space. You were on the wrong side of the road, cutting into an area already reserved and had a traffic policeman seen you you would have been fined. Whatever chemistry was working in you bubbled upwards and you deliberately usurped the parking lot of the smaller car. You claimed you didn't like the make of the car and the occupants looked as if they had dissenting political opinions from yours. Furthermore, you explained, as you twisted the wheel and backed into the narrow corridor between a large Buick and a medium-sized Pontiac, there had been no ladies in the little car so let *them* walk through the dust to the club entrance rather than us. This was merely preliminary rumblings of thunder to the actual incident itself.

You felt, in reality, a little foolish and turned to the novia for confirmation; obediently, she backed you up; you were a wonderful driver, it was marvellous the way you'd obtained the parking space, the men in the small car had looked revolting.

We walked in an uncomfortable silence to the tennis court, the victors, thanks to a big car and numerical superiority, of a parking space over a small car.

The bowl-shaped stadium was crowded, the audience already whistling and stamping with impatience for the match to begin. The sun beat down mercilessly; far to the east a storm was brewing and the air was heavy and ominous. Men had loosened their ties and rolled up their shirt sleeves, discarding their jackets for greater comfort; the dresses of the women stuck damply to their bodies; even the young ball-boys who usually clowned in the smooth center-court before a match drooped wearily in the scant shade of one side of the arena. You led the way to where you saw three seats together and we climbed over legs and hats to reach them.

Your uneasiness was contagious; your novia shifted her position on the bench fifty times, giggled at the low-toned jokes you told her, accepted countless Coca-Colas from you; you sat between her and me, addressing me only to place bets on the players as the games mounted up and rolled into three sets, then four and at last five. Between sets you rose and flexed your muscles, left us each time to tear off to greet people, the last time staying for several games seated beside the stooge, as much of a tennis-fan as you. You were displeased with yourself, the novia's comfort was insufficient, you went for assuagement to the stooge. I saw your two heads together, his blond and yours black, not observing the match, and I could gather you were explaining in detail about the parking space; I saw him nod and his teeth glinted in a smile. Reassured, you returned to us.

The championship was decided after the fifth set, both contestants gasping in the heat. They were scheduled to play the finals of the doubles championship against each other immediately following the conclusion of their singles, but they were so weak that a three-quarter-of-an-hour pause was announced between matches. The two players, leaning heavily on their trainers, stumbled from the court. The audience rose and fussed, stirring discontentedly in the oven-like heat. The cup, too heavy to be carried off, was left standing on the sand of the court, shining blindingly in the blazing light.

"It won't be much of a fight in the doubles," I observed. "Two of the four players are finished before they start. Why don't we skip it," I suggested, "and go home and cool off? It's going to rain soon anyway and they'll probably have to postpone the match."

"It won't rain before midnight," you said, and rushed off to greet still another friend. Your shirt stuck to your back and the glistening sweat-beads had gathered in the eyebrows and along the upper lip of your novia.

"Can't you persuade him to take us home and be comfortable?" I asked her, as she mopped her face with a thin, lacy handkerchief that could not absorb the perspiration.

You bounced back in time to hear the last.

"Go home, go home?" you said. "But who wants to go home? We came to see the tennis and it isn't over yet!"

We faced each other briefly in the heat and stink of the stadium. Unknowingly, you were massaging your rump where it was sore from the two and a half hours on the hard stone bench. You were fighting against me, not because you wanted to see the doubles but because you did not want me to have my way, even if my way were the sanest and most comfortable. You had to persist in the day's line of stubborn conduct which you had inaugurated with the affair of the parking space.

"All right," I said. "You stay. I'll take a taxi home."

I shook hands with you in saying good-bye, offering you a last-minute opportunity to be sensible. There was, of course, no possibility of obtaining a taxi, that had been a polite lie on my part and, as the house was a short ten minutes' drive from the court, you could easily drive me there and return with still twenty minutes to spare from the long pause between matches. Your novia, sensing something wrong, came to help you.

"And with gasoline so hard to get," she inserted in an attempt to rescue you from whatever muddle you'd fallen into, "probably a taxi is best."

All small, common phrases, a quick, light discussion of comfort and desires and yet containing the very essence of our relationships to each other. You had, to put it bluntly, made an offer and not held to it, which from a point of view of manners was an offence and from a practical viewpoint was an error in strategy, for you were still too green and untried in the business (where I had a powerful say) to be able to afford such nonchalance towards me.

In parting, you beamed upon me, a great, toothy pretended smile; knowing you were desperately in the wrong you wanted to show me how unaffected you were.

There was no taxi, as I had known, and I walked slowly through the steaming sun to the station and boarded the Sunday suburban local, jamming myself into second class —first class was full up—against the half-naked garlic-breathing Italians, the Spanish women laden with presents of live chickens and squashed grapes.

The suburban stations slipped by with increasing numbers of Sunday gallants crowding into the coach to swell the tooth-picking, nose-cleaning, suspender-snapping mob. It was an expensive trip for me; my newest dress, worn in your honor, was grape-stained, and chicken droppings dribbled down upon my shoes.

In a measure I was pleased, even delighted, with what you had done. I wanted you to suffer, and how exquisitely pleasant to know in advance that you *would* suffer down to the last refinement of knowing *I* knew. I foresaw with relish the hot, sleepless night through which you would toss protestingly, scolding yourself and complaining against me.

She railroaded me into it, you would tell yourself. *She's always so damned quick. Before you know what's happened, it's over with. She always strikes when one isn't looking. She didn't give me a chance to offer to drive her home.*

Then there was the business of telephoning an apology, the least you could have done by way of excusing yourself.

I couldn't telephone, you told yourself. *I was out until midnight, dancing. You can't telephone people at midnight.*

The real reason you wouldn't telephone was because we were to lunch together the following day in town and you hoped everything could be settled then. You planned to play innocent, to be solicitous, to gloss over matters or simply, if necessary, to ignore, and yet you knew, in the very moment you had smiled the make-believe toothy smile at me, that we weren't going to lunch together, that the telephone would ring in the morning in your office and I would break the engagement. By inaction you hoped, rather pathetically, to avoid.

Then you told yourself you'd be damned if you'd let me bother you; you'd think of your novia, but that did not erase me from your mind. Furthermore, in telling yourself you would *not* think of me, what were you doing *except* thinking of me?

You lay in bed in the murky, stifling dark and could not sleep. I owed you money because of the bets we had made during the tennis match, a fiver because I had backed the wrong player and a tenner for claiming it would rain before midnight. Everything was uncomfortable about lying in bed; you tossed off the light blanket and then the crumpled sheet. Exactly on this bed you had lain with me. At night, before you went to sleep, it was usually pleasant to remember that; tonight it was so much unsuppressible torture.

You rehearsed the afternoon of that event; it was already more than half a year ago. In an unseasonal heat wave, winter had been eclipsed, and the day had been soft and warm;

you were running away from me, the initial escape that introduced a long series of similar ones, into a yachting weekend, and I entered your flat simultaneously with the janitor who was taking your valises down to your car. Where you had located friends rich enough to have a yacht and nouveauriche enough to need young bachelors such as you as attractions for more important guests, I did not know, but I quickly saw you were prepared for every contingency the yacht might produce; for four days you took three suitcases.

"Have you decided you really want to stay my lover? Always?" I had asked you as I lay in your arms on the bed.

"Of course I want to be your lover. Always."

"Have you decided then you love me?"

"Do women know what love is?" you had countered, curious. "Because men don't. We know passion, we know sex, we know tenderness, we know desire, we know protection, we need companionship, humor, and now and then we must be whipped. Is that love?"

"I don't think women know what love is," I had replied.

You looked surprised.

"Then why are they always talking about it?" you had inquired reasonably.

"What else shall they talk of?"

You surveyed me a moment and then you had said, almost fiercely as if to stop any contention on my part:

"I want things *my way,* do you understand, *my way.* I won't be ordered about. I want *my way.*"

"Fine," I had agreed lazily. "Explain to me what you mean by 'your way.' So far it has been nothing but an idleness, a procrastination, an uncertainty. Have you really a way, or are you all confusion and fog?"

"There is a way for me," you had replied; "perhaps I've missed it. It's difficult for me to be as positive as you are. How can anybody be so sure of what he wants?"

I had considered saying "Self-preservation"; instead I had found it wise to say "Kiss me."

On your bed, in your arms, above you, beneath you, my skin under your hands, my hair against your face, my mouth next to yours, and to where did it lead? To a damp summer night during the length and breadth of which you relived, like some perpetual-motion machine, scenes from which there was no escape.

Then, preceded by a stiffening of the breeze in the trees and the louder swish and lap of the river a few blocks away, came the rain, a light, steady summer stream, refreshing nothing, merely wetting everything, close and cloying. The rain was like sex itself, soft, satisfying and sleep-producing without provoking more than a temporary stimulus.

She owes me a tenner, you thought. *What time is it?*

It was half-past three in the morning.

Well, I've won the tenner from her, you told yourself grimly, but these were all surface thoughts for what you were really saying was something entirely different. You were speaking, actually, in three layers, something like a sandwich. The top layer was your whisper, *I've won the tenner from her,* the second layer was your conscience, *I won't think of her any more,* and the third layer, identical with the romantic wish, was reciting again and again like an

118

overwound phonograph, the anonymous poetic lines, unconsciously altering their tense, *Western wind which now doth blow, so the small rain down can rain, Christ, that I in my bed, had my love in my arms again!* It was half-past four when you heard the rain stop, and you twisted and turned in your sleep.

The following morning was again hot and heavy. The sun quickly dried the soaked grass and the over-worked, poorly fed milk-horses stumbled and fell from sunstroke in the streets and lay panting on the hot asphalt, too stricken to move.

You answered my telephone call to your office with simulated cheerfulness.

"Something unexpected has turned up," I said into the mouthpiece, "and I'm afraid I won't be able to come to town to lunch with you today, much as I had looked forward to it."

"What, what?" you shouted from the receiving end. "I can't hear. I got only the first part. You can't have lunch with me. I'm sorry."

"You'll forgive me for letting you know at the eleventh hour?" I went on.

"Of course I forgive you," you said with the magnanimity of the guilty. You hesitated an instant. "Anything bad?"

"No," I assured you. "Not at all."

"Nothing bad," you mused, and then, finding no words to express the fact that you realized that I was breaking the engagement (as you knew I would) because of your yesterday's impossible behavior, and that this was your last chance to redeem yourself by saying, "Listen, I'm an ass, overlook my idiocy," or, "Did you get home all right yesterday," or even, "I'm sorry about yesterday," you produced, instead, in the most significant and portentous tone you could command, the all-expressive sound of "hmmmmmmm."

Replacing the receiver, I shook my head at the liver-shaped black French telephone and wondered if your vanity had become so colossal that you planned to protract a moment's mistake into a life-long social sin. Preparing to go through the garden to cut flowers for the house I chanced, by some unknown compulsion, to look at the palm of my right hand. I had grown so accustomed to the small, irate rash that slashed across it that I had come to manipulate my hand in such a way that the dried skin no longer caught on sheer fabrics or molested me. Now I noticed, with considerable surprise, that this rash had disappeared; the palm was as before, simply and severely lined with nothing unusual to distinguish it except perhaps that on the fat, fleshy outer part there was a slight mark where the rash had been, as if new lines had appeared in the hand *under* the skin.

It was not long, of course, before this lapse of yours was forgiven and you came with the novia to the house for the summer weekends, swimming and playing tennis. During the week I saw little of you, and then only by chance. Although you were at my service over Saturdays and Sundays, I took it for granted that, in these hot months, you would devote yourself during the week to the novia. People began to talk of you and her as a pair, and I learned that many of the friends you made in my house invited you both together to their houses for parties with younger people than I.

Between the novia and myself there was an undercurrent of something foul and dangerous. The novia resented my influence over you and instead of profiting from it she fought against it. Over the weekends she was continually asking you to take her riding, or drive her here or there for a visit, or come on an errand with her; all sorts of excuses to separate you from me. You were impatient with her tricks, not realizing they were ruses.

Outwardly, the novia and I were great friends. It struck me sometimes, and disagreeably, that I was almost old enough to be her mother and I would look surreptitiously at her, considering her as a daughter. I found her wanting, or perhaps I valued the daughter I might have had too highly.

She never came to me for advice, nor would she talk to me in private. Her cordiality, like mine, was for public consumption. I was aware she was afraid and resentful of me, but I doubt if she ever felt that I had anything but affection for her. Whatever suspicions she might have entertained regarding my relationship with you, she never once had the opportunity to prove them justified.

On the whole, the novia was restrained when she was with you, almost blatantly careful not to give me a clue (or so she thought) concerning the depths of her feeling for you. Demonstrativeness was, to her thwarted and miserly old-maid's nature, something vulgar and definitely out-of-place. Either she forgot or never knew how much can be revealed in a glance and a gesture, the intonation of a phrase, an oblique reference. She imposed upon herself a kind of hands-off attitude while, at the same time, glowering at whoever dared to approach you and dispute her possession of you.

Inevitably the day came when my presence goaded her beyond endurance and she flung discretion impatiently from her, like a garment too heavy to wear, and made a disastrous attempt to show me once and for all that you belonged to her.

Possibly the heat was the really responsible agent. I had been obliged to go to town on a sweltering Wednesday afternoon, and walking along the steaming streets I encountered the novia, hatless and dishevelled, a strand of hair straggling damply behind one ear.

"Come and have a cool lemonade with me," I invited, tucking my arm under her elbow and drawing her into the slight shade of a nearby awning. "You look hot."

She hesitated a moment and then told me, with a hint of triumph in her voice, that she had no time; she had asked you to her flat at five-thirty for a mint-julep and she didn't want to be late. Tardily, she realized that she must, of course, invite me, too; what would a respectable widow think—and recount in future gossip—if she boasted of being alone with you in her apartment and yet refused so friendly a chaperonage as mine. It would have been better to have foregone the victory of informing me you were coming to her and have had the pleasure of keeping you to herself but, having shown her cards, as it were, she had to play her hand, **and** she could only add in a vinegary voice:

"Won't you come and join us?"

With malice, I accepted, and we took a taxi together to her apartment, a group of dully furnished dark-brown rooms that exuded an indefinable mixture of cold cream and that sweetish, almost etherish aroma of female. She left me in her living-room to go fuss over the juleps in her pantry and, rather than help her crack ice and pound mint leaves, I sat quietly cooling off on a pale-green satin sofa that looked borrowed from the nearest brothel. She had barely set the drinks on the cocktail table, combed her disordered hair and washed her hands when you rang the bell and bounded in, complaining at the heat and shouting "Hello" all in one breath. Your surprise and delight at unexpectedly finding me in the dreary apartment were evident to the dullest onlooker, and there was nothing unobservant about the quick darts of the novia's eyes. You flung yourself beside me on the sofa, looked into my face and observed:

"You always look warm and inviting when you should, and cool and reposed when you should. What's your secret?" Without waiting for an answer, you rushed on, "That's a pretty dress," and your voice was genuinely admiring. You turned to the novia and said pettishly, "Why don't you ever wear something like that? Something with lots of color to it?" and you waved a careless hand at my light silk suit that cost double as much as all the novia's clothes combined.

Angry and humiliated, the novia slammed a sugarbowl onto the cocktail table and began to ladle sugar into your glass. Feeling me watching her, she explained, as people explain about their pet puppy dogs:

"He likes his julep sweet."

She was so pleased at being able to serve you that I bit my lip in sheer embarrassment and looked away, hoping you would say nothing but, bobbing forward on the sofa, you began to remonstrate.

"What makes you think I like it sweet? This is the first mint-julep you've ever served me. I don't like sweet things!"

Crashing about her ears, came the structure the novia had built to convince me that taking juleps together in her apartment was an established custom between you and her. You had not meant to be cruel; you were merely unaware that there was any friction between the novia and me. I was always relaxed, smiling and pleasant with the novia, and if she became tense and nervous you could hardly be expected to associate that with my ever-obliging, sociable presence.

Thoroughly rattled, the novia made a false move and your frosted mint-julep glass tipped over, clinking the ice along the mirrored table-top, the bourbon spreading darkly. The novia fumbled hurriedly with the ineffectual squares of linen that were cocktail napkins, I dabbed at the mess with my handkerchief and you went to the pantry for a towel.

The novia apologized stiffly. You pushed her into a chair, placed her glass in her hands and said,

"Take it easy for a moment. The heat must have got you. I'll go make my own in the kitchen."

"But, darling," the novia cried out in anguish, the endearment coming naturally to her, "there's no more bourbon! The bottle's finished. I didn't expect . . ." and she looked at me, leaving her sentence unfinished; she hadn't expected an extra guest was what she meant to say. "Here." She proffered her glass to you. "You can have mine. I don't really want it, anyway."

Exasperated, you refused her drink curtly, saying the one thing she obviously needed most in the world to pull herself together was a strong drink. I hoped you would have the good sense not to say you would share *my* drink but would, instead, accept part of the novia's and give her at least the infinitesimal pleasure of sharing her glass with you, but you reseated yourself beside me and asked calmly, stretching out your hand,

"Can I share yours with you?"

I wanted to leave, heat and mint-juleps notwithstanding; I felt the accumulation of slight calamities before so alert a witness as myself was really more punishment than the novia deserved for her silliness. Once I had gone, she could throw herself into your arms, have a satisfying cry on your shoulder and conceivably you might take her to the bedroom. I drank rapidly and then thrust the glass at you, saying it was all yours. But when I rose to go, you jumped up and offered to drive me home or to wherever I was going; you had your car parked downstairs.

The room was dark with the shades drawn against the city's summer glare and in the artificial dusk we felt rather than saw each other's reactions.

I acquiesced and you wheeled on the novia.

"Listen," you ordered; "take a cool bath and put on a nice dress. Something lively. When I come back we'll go to an air-cooled movie and then have an air-cooled dinner. You're all on edge. How will that be?" You spoke as if she were a particularly retarded child who needed special handling.

She should have been delighted with the prospect of an evening with you but you had spoiled it for her by your insistence on escorting me home. She understood very well that it was not mere politeness that prompted your solicitude; you wanted to be alone with me for the sheer joy of being alone with me, furthermore, your conscience still troubled you about the episode of the tennis-match and you sought to make amends. The novia's tired, badgered mind immediately imagined a variety of erotic scenes; bleached with jealousy, her eyes bright with misery, the novia asked how long you would take. Something of her wretchedness must have communicated itself to you because you put an arm around her shoulder, more like a brother than a lover I was quick to notice, and assured her in the absent tone men use when lying to their wives, that you'd be back "in no time." She leaned against you for an instant and then drew away; a bit of color had come into her face.

I was silent as you helped me into the car, and suddenly you asked:

"Is there something wrong with you, too? Or is it my fault?"

"Why don't you buy a flower, a corsage for her?" I suggested. "If you're taking her out tonight you might as well do it with all the trimmings."

You looked sideways at me and I thought perhaps you were going to protest at my meddling, but you only said, by way of argument:

"But I wanted to take the river road back to avoid the town. It's cooler."

"You can buy it now on the way out," I commented.

"Oh, all right." You shrugged in agreement and set the car into motion, pulling up at a florist's a few blocks distant and actually running into the store.

Through the plate-glass window I saw you select two orchids and then begin that loose-jointed search in your pockets typical to men who have misplaced their money. Suddenly you clapped a hand to your forehead, spoke sharply to the salesgirl and dashed out to me as I waited in the car. Behind you, I noticed, the salesgirl was returning one of the orchids to the mammoth glass icebox.

You were red in the face and sweat stood out on your upper lip. You spoke rapidly.

"Listen," you said. "I've done something stupid. Either I've lost my wallet or it slipped out on the sofa while we were having drinks. Could you lend me a tenner?"

"Of course," I said, opening my bag; and, as I handed you the notes I inquired why you had bought *two* orchids?

You grabbed the notes, threw me a look of intense irritation and replied snappily:

"One was for you. But I can't very well ask you to pay for your own orchid, can I?"

I held the transparent cellophane box with its exotic and expensive content gingerly on my lap and I wondered how you would explain, should the novia have found your wallet on the sofa, that you could buy orchids on credit, without a cent in your pockets, at a florist's you never patronized. The novia would guess the orchid had been bought with my money and what had been meant as a pleasure-giving compliment for her would turn into a bitter barb. I sighed, dismissing her from my thoughts with the reflection that we all have our bad days and this one was surely hers.

CHAPTER EIGHT

Cutting the roses in the garden, I reflected that wealth is not a matter of accumulation—whether of money or affection—but consists, rather, in being content with what is obtainable. Since man is, by nature, avaricious, he can never decide that what is obtainable is sufficient to give satisfaction; satisfaction, he tells himself, comes only when he has more—more money, more power, more love.

I did not want you to love me more; of what use is melodramatic idolization? That you loved me was enough. It seemed unimportant to me to endeavor to measure the "how much" of your love as if it were a cooking recipe that needed a particular amount of butter and sugar to be acceptable. You felt otherwise. You ran away from me again, precipitately, in some kind of attempt to divine the meaning of this attachment between us; or perhaps you tried to break it during the six or seven days' holiday you claimed you needed.

You came late to a luncheon appointment with me, breathless with your decision, and announced at once that you would go with the stooge for a week's motor-trip to the south. You lowered your eyes while you spoke, breaking a toothpick in three equal parts and examining the splinters as they lay before you on the tablecloth. When I refused any comment, you threw up your head, like a frisky colt up to some mischief, and asked:

"Are you jealous?"

My first reaction had been one of resentment: how could you bear to go from me, I had thought irritably; but immediately this was followed by a feeling of triumph: you were afraid of me and were running away, the better to run back of course. Then the fact that you were going with the stooge occupied my attention; why didn't you go alone, why must you always lean on someone? With these fireworks of thought I had had, literally, no time to answer you. Now your question threw a different and unexpected light on my reactions.

"Why should I be jealous?" I asked slowly. "I know the south. I've motored all through it, and once is enough. The roads are bad and there is too much dust and heat at this time of year. It's hardly what I would pick as a pleasure-trip."

"Aside from all that," you said almost eagerly, "are you jealous?"

I found, with a shock, that I *was* jealous, not of your trip, but of the fact that somehow—through what chain of fortunate circumstances I did not know—somehow you were able to recede into that teen-age irresponsibility that I had left behind. For the first time in my life I felt old. You wanted to go on an uncomfortable trip, not merely to escape from me, but also just for the hell of it; you wanted to cut up, to rough it, to speed over the open country, howling like a wild Indian at the top of your lungs, riding a bucking Buick instead of a bucking bronco, but riding in any event; you wanted to swap silly jokes with the stooge, years younger than you, you wanted to get drunk in some small-town hotel, you wanted to feel free and young and unattached, leaving behind you knowledge, wisdom, experience and the weight of adulthood. I was fiercely, wildly, jealous of this. What right had you to do this when I couldn't?

"She is jealous, she is jealous," you said, leaning across the table towards me. "She is jealous of me, of the open car, of the time away from her, of my friend!" You were grinning with pleasure and your eyes snapped in nasty exhilaration.

"I'll get you for that!" I promised bitterly. "I'll punish you!" My voice vibrated with anger through the empty restaurant. "I'll make it rain!" I threatened. "You'll see, I'll turn the roads to mud!"

You threw yourself back in your seat, your eyes narrowed, grinning wickedly at me, mocking my ineffectual, impossible threat.

"Jealous!" you taunted. "You are completely jealous!"

"I'll make it rain!" I cried in an excess of folly. "You'll see! I will! I will!"

I left you at the door of the restaurant and walked slowly through the city streets towards the station to take the suburban local home. I should not permit myself to be jealous. I had been given in abundance what others spend their lives in attaining. I expected to make retribution, but I had conceived of the retribution as something big and final, such as an early death, and not as a series of inconveniences in the nature of being unable to return to adolescence. I doubt that man is made for abundance; man is at his best at struggling and at his worst in leisure.

By abundance I mean possession, everything which the other fellow might possibly want: position, power, love, wealth.

Given abundance, for what does one live? Has one been made an experiment of by the Lord, a sort of white rat about which the Divine says: "Let's surfeit it and watch its reaction." Logically, I imagine, I should lie down and die, there being nothing more for me to want and negative motives being inadequate to maintain life. "I don't desire, I don't struggle"; if one can truthfully say this, isn't one dead? Or, by a huge joke, is it possible that one is in heaven where everything is reputed peace?

How disappointed you would have been had I not been

jealous! That I should dare to endeavor to live unemotionally is something you resented. Men *want* women to suffer preferably because of them; it's gratifying. If I won't suffer, I'm exasperating. Emotions are so much simpler than thought to deal with; why complicate?

Yet, emotions are dangerous, for they are cloudy and untrue and as a consequence they lead to hopeless misunderstandings, unrest, dissatisfaction, bitterness. Time is too precious to be squandered by indulging in such unrest or any of the other end-products of emotionalism. Your argument always had been that only through extremes of feeling can "the blood be heated" (your own words). Most likely; but how is hot blood helpful? Is one any nearer serenity, is one any quieter, any clearer, any surer, any calmer? And if one is *not* (and how can one be, trotting about with a boiler blazing in the veins?) how is one any different from the Great Mob which surges around in storm and exaggerations and futility? Of what possible use are emotions? And if they are of no use, they must be, like all other useless attributes in the world, pure art. Then, the highest art would be to obtain the most difficult emotion, the one that comprises all the others. Which emotion is that? Humility? Is humility an emotion? If it should be, and one could achieve it, what purpose to retreat into the muck and passion of unrest?

The morning you and the stooge drove off into the country was warm and bright, the perfect day for touring in an open car. I was frantic with annoyance; how could nature so betray me? Was I not the more mature and disciplined

133

personality of the two of us? Was I not entitled to a reward for my clarity and vision? I flung myself into the garden to torture myself with the warmth of the sun and the sweetness of the air. In my rage, I looked at the ground instead of the sky, protesting to the grass until, dull and distant, I heard it, the long, low, lovely roll of summer thunder, and I raised my head to search the sky; from the south, piling up dark and threatening, were the heavy thunderheads. Even as I stood on the lawn I could feel the air freshening, and I saw the wheel of the windmill turn from the east to the south and begin to spin steadily. I ran to the barometer in the pump-house and read it avidly; it was low, the black pointer standing on "Tempest." I watched the dark storm-clouds approach and when they overtook the sun and cast everything in shadow I sighed with relief and gratefulness. Here was the omen, the unmistakable sign, that you should not have run away from me; here was the announcement, written all over the heavens for you to read, that I was stronger than you. I had said I would make it rain to punish you, and the tempest was coming out of the south, out of the region where you were going. I watched the first drops, large as quarters, fall on the flagstones of the garden path. Voodoo, I thought, and stood in the rain, hot with excitement in the cold polar wind, uneasy and even ashamed now that I had obtained what I had called a half an hour earlier my just due.

The bad weather lasted five days, breaking a long drought that had brought the farming industries of the country to the verge of ruin; from the south came reports of floods. The sixth day the rain came only in gusts and flurries, whirled about by a strong gale; the day you were due back in town, the swollen, grey clouds scudded steadily across the skies but no rain fell. You were twenty-four hours late, held up, according to a telegram you sent the old lawyer, by storms, and when you finally reached the office, pale, hollow-eyed from strenuous driving and snivelling with a running head cold, the sun came out in full strength, the weather turned pleasant and warm. By accident, I happened to see you in the afternoon, just as the business was closing. I had gone to town and was about to cross the heavily trafficked street to pick up my monthly statement from the office when I saw a mud-splattered, filthy open touring car edge down the street towards the office building. I recognized the stooge at the wheel; his blond thatch was unmistakable. Passers-by turned to stare at the car, it was so stained and grimed that it was doubly conspicuous. The stooge crawled along by the curb until you ran out of the building and threw yourself heavily into the front seat beside him. You sneezed as you settled yourself, once, twice and then a third time. As the car drove off I saw you pull out of your pocket a large white handkerchief and lean forward in your seat the better to have a really good blow. Thus returns the modern adventurer to the comforts of civilization.

Of a shrewd turn of mind, you capitalized on your cold, but only after a suitable interval had elapsed. One day you did not come to the office and there was much fuss and inquiry about what might have happened to you. I telephoned you. You sounded subdued and a bit hoarse and asked me to come and see you.

Most men are, I think, far more apt to be hypochondriacs than women. One theory explains this by pointing out that women are much more used to pain and as a consequence they can bear it better. I maintain this is ridiculous; a woman suffers as much as a man does from a wound or a cut or an infection; is the quality of her flesh and blood, after all, any different? Then, too, men are notoriously fond of being babied, whereas women, all too close, as a rule, to this babying business, have small patience with it. In any case, you wanted sympathy. I gathered you were again in some sort of quarrel with your novia or else you would not have called on me; you would have preferred to maintain the policy of ignoring me until you could find an adequate excuse not to.

The sun was streaming into your bedroom when I entered, admitted by your attractive mulatto maid. I was immediately struck by the fact that you had shaved for me and then I understood that you were no more ill than I was; the whole scene was an elaborate fake. Your pale-rose pajamas were fresh and uncreased, the sheets smooth and unwrinkled. I sat on the edge of your bed and shook my head at you.

"Well," I asked, aware of the age-old wish of men to be nursed by their mistresses. "Well, is it as you want?"

"Don't be subtle," you replied, closing your eyes in feigned weariness.

"Don't evade," I retorted. "You've played this scene a hundred times. You created it on the trip as soon as you caught cold. Are you satisfied with it?"

With a quick and unexpected sweep of your arms you pulled me so that I lay over you.

"It's going to be as I've imagined it," you said.

I began to laugh in your arms, my mouth next to your smooth cheek.

"Are you playing games with me?" you asked suspiciously, uneasy at my laughter.

It seemed to me utterly impossible ever to explain to you. The more words I found to tell you, the less sense I made to you, the more involved and remote I became. How could I convince you there was no need for me to sleep with you and yet show you that intercourse between us was always, every minute possible, delightful and superfluous? Your conceptions were too direct; "I love," was your credo, "therefore I possess." What did I care for all your pantings and exertions? How easy it would have been to say, "I love, I'll copulate until I can't stand the sight of him any more, until I love no more." This overemphasis, this exaggeration of the importance of the sexual act was so much nonsense to me. Lucky people, I thought, who could settle their love affairs by a dose of erotic exercises. Had I loved you for your bodily attractions I should never have been bothered by you, for each time I had physical need of you I could have come to your apartment, climbed into your bed and said, in whatever phrase I cared to contrive, the equivalent of "Come along, get going." Sexual need of you was the very least of our relationship. I did not need to sublimate, even that common outlet was denied me; how is it possible to sublimate when there are no restrictions, either on oneself or the beloved?

The peril of our relationship was the uncanny, unending knowledge that I had of you and that I feared you might come to have of me. Is there anyone in this world who could stand to have his mind read as easily as an open book, or, more aptly, as pictorially as a movie? How many times do we not say to the person with whom we are dealing, "I wish to God I knew what you are thinking!" Imagine the disadvantage of having one's thoughts clear to the other. One has no privacy and no mystery; one is the most naked of public whores.

"I'm not playing games with you," I replied, kissed you and freed myself from the nervous grasp of your arms. "Tomorrow you'll feel all right," I predicted. "Come and play tennis this weekend."

You came for the Saturday afternoon tennis, bringing me an armful of expensive flowers. I was amused to see you thought that peace and goodwill could be bought, like so much liverwurst at the grocer's.

I think that the downward course of your business career began that day. After the tennis, in that long pause over cooling drinks and a congenial rehash of the game, set by set, when the body is pleasantly tired and the mind devoid of any thought, there came a long-distance business telephone-call on an emergency situation that had arisen in one of the subsidiary companies, one of those tedious, annoying complications that spoil the businessman's and his legal adviser's weekend as effectively as a cloudburst spoils a racetrack.

My elderly lawyer, weekending at the house, took you with him into the library and gave you instructions on work to be done the following day. As his assistant, you were not given the alluring plums of the work, but the unflattering, essential and boring details. I heard you hesitate as you accepted the responsibility for these details and I followed your movements as you left the library. You sauntered into the vestibule, unconscious of my near presence, and I heard you telephone to the stooge, tell him what you were entrusted to do and ask him to do it for you.

"I've got a date to go picnicking tomorrow," you explained, sotto voce. "If I don't go she'll think . . . oh, you know. Women. Always jumping to conclusions. And listen, I'll do the same for you if ever you want, you know that."

As you turned from the vestibule to cross the hall and so go out to the terrace, you met me. We confronted each other in silence; even in the gloom of the late afternoon I could see the dark-red blood rush to your face. You looked at me defiantly.

I brushed past you, half angry that you were so foolish as to place your pleasure above your career when with a career you could permit yourself far greater pleasures, half glad that you were fool enough to make vital mistakes.

Ordinarily this incident might have gone unperceived, but on Sunday morning there was another emergency call and the plans of the previous day had to be altered. I listened while my lawyer telephoned your number, and in the silence of the library I heard your mulatto maid's voice, with its light, peculiar accent, say metallically through the receiver that you had gone picnicking for the day and wouldn't be back before midnight.

When Christmas came, a few weeks later, and salary raises were awarded the junior executives, you were passed over, despite your being the most able. In justice to you, I must admit you did not complain; you felt you had deserved the slight. Although I noticed all this at the time, it was only considerably later that I made use of the business as an instrument for furthering your destruction.

Very likely the realization that you were committing a series of errors led you to commit still one more. Early in the New Year you telephoned to ask me to come to your flat at four o'clock on a Wednesday afternoon because you had something "highly important" to tell me. Your voice was so pompous that my curiosity was avid for details and I came punctually, anxious to know what deviltry you had cooked up. The day was swelteringly hot; the shutters in your living-room were closed, producing a strange tomb-like light. You were in shirt sleeves and obviously ill-at-ease. I understood at once that whatever you were about to tell me was supposed to produce a cataclysmic effect on me. Hastily, I reviewed in my mind what news you would consider disturbing to me: your departure for another country, your decision to commit suicide within the next twenty-four hours, your marriage. That was it, of course. Your vague period of "being engaged to" the novia was concluded and you and your novia had finally settled upon a date for the wedding. I wondered, rapidly, if you would like an electric phonograph as a wedding present or whether your novia would consider that a one-sided gift as she did not care too much for music.

"Here I am," I said casually, throwing my wide-brimmed hat on the neat table that served you for playing cards and breakfasting. "What is it you want to tell me?"

I stood by the bookshelves, near the partition that housed your precious Ming vase; you perched on the corner of your desk opposite me, swinging your leg. Possibly it is characteristic of the difference in our temperaments that I like to give and take my news, good or bad, standing up while you prefer to be seated.

"I'm sorry, but you won't like this," you said, and I had the fleeting suspicion you were enjoying this preliminary to what you thought would be a mortal blow. "I'm going to marry."

"It's about time," I agreed, nodding. "You've been putting it off long enough. When is it to be?"

You considered me in surprise, obviously crestfallen that your announcement had been, as you understood from my reaction, not merely anticipated, but taken for granted.

"We're going to be married right away," you insisted. "Within the next two weeks. More or less."

"And the newspaper job in the States?" I ventured, for I was well aware of the interminable bickering about careers, the novia claiming hers more important than yours simply to make you think more highly of her.

"Oh," you said crisply, "of course she'll go to New York right away and see if she can get a special job as foreign correspondent down here. In the meantime I'll find a house out of town and move . . ." you trailed off, for I had taken the Ming vase in my hands and was turning it over and over idly, feeling it, scrutinizing it, familiar though it was. What devil possessed me I don't know, but suddenly I threw it into the air, heard you suck in your breath, caught it expertly and replaced it on its carved lacquer foot. "Why did you do that?" you asked me and came swinging across the room, looking hot and foolish with outrage.

"I don't know," I told you truthfully. "I just saw the vase and remembered what it meant and I thought this would be a propitious moment to treat it lightly."

"But don't you care about my marrying?" you demanded.

"What difference would it make in our lives together?" I asked.

You looked aggrieved and astonished; the pious, moral expression I so detested spread like spilled slops over your features.

"But don't you realize that then we wouldn't be able to see each other any more?" you protested.

"No," I answered shortly. "I don't realize anything of the sort. On the contrary, if you take a house out of town it will probably be nearer me and I shall see a good deal more of you than otherwise, and with less risk of gossip."

"But I won't want to see you any more. I want to be faithful to my wife!"

"What has your wife got to do with you and me?" I asked.

You placed your hands on my shoulders in the familiar gesture you used towards me whenever you reached, in our discussions, an impasse.

"Will you be a different man when you are married?" I persisted. "Will you change so much that you will no longer want what you have valued so highly before the marriage?"

I felt your fingers playing with my hair; a slight, sardonic smile came to your mouth and your eyes searched mine unblinkingly.

"Why do men never marry the women they love?" I asked you. "Why do they insist upon marrying the women they *think* they should love?"

I expected you to overwhelm me with an avalanche of platitudes to the contrary. "But I love her with all my heart!" "But men love their wives!" "But I'm marrying her because I want to, for love!" I suppose you, too, had realized that if you loved your wife, seeing me would be a matter of supreme indifference to you. So long as it was not, what sort of love were you offering her? You had no necessity to marry for any reason except for love alone. You reached for your jacket, wriggled into it, shut the few lattices that were still open in the shutters and moved towards the door, picking up my hat as you passed the table.

"I'll drive you to town," you offered, "if you're going there. It's Wednesday. That's your town day, isn't it?"

We did not speak to each other during the drive. What was there to say? "I hope you'll be happy, darling," was hardly in keeping with my philosophy that people have no business expecting long-term happiness as if it were a gilt-edged bond on the emotional stock market. "I hope you'll make a go of it, darling," was equally silly, for people live alone all their lives and not to make a go of a marriage is a sign of laziness; what is so very difficult in two people living together? Only patience, discipline and a certain minimum of tolerance are needed. "You've broken my heart, darling," was pure trash; your matrimonial intentions did not touch my heart. "Darling, I'll love you forever, no matter whom you marry," was so much idiocy, for we both knew that I would love you only as long as I permitted myself this luxury, as it diverted me to love you. "How could you do this to me, darling?" would have made us laugh, for you had done nothing to me at all.

As we drove to town I began to feel sleepy, for our interview had been a strain; I had had to be alert and the effort had been tiring. I thought of my little Biblical phrase and grinned ironically: *He giveth his beloved sleep,* I quoted to myself; he driveth his beloved to the market, I substituted. What about her, I wondered. Does she give her beloved sleep? Were you the exceptional man that you wanted sleep, or were all men equally tired, desiring respite? As I ambled through these thoughts, their significance suddenly struck me. *Sleep,* I thought, *sleep has a double meaning. Sleep means death.* "To die is but to sleep," I whispered; from Verdi back to Shakespeare, how many poets had maintained this? *She giveth her beloved sleep, I give my beloved sleep. I kill my beloved.* I looked at your hand upon the wheel and it occurred to me that we often speak of different limbs being asleep: "My foot has gone to sleep, or my arm." But instead of the foot or arm being devoid of sensation, this "being asleep" is accompanied by a disconcerting feeling of prickling or of shooting pains. Perhaps that was the essential difference between the temporary living sleep and the eternal dead sleep, that in the living sleep the body could still react and in death the body disintegrated and disappeared.

Your hand left the wheel and closed over mine.

"What are you whispering?" you asked. "Have you taken up talking to yourself?"

"Yes and no," I answered. "Yes because I'm always talking to myself, but no because it hasn't been aloud, so far." Then I stopped short for I realized I was giving you the sort of answer you had already given me.

"Ah-ha!" you said with satisfaction. "So you, too, have come to the yes-and-no answer. You have found out that nothing is ever categorically negative or positive."

With the exception, I thought, of death. Death is quite positive; possibly truth, too; but there must always be an element of doubt about the truth because although *we* may know it, how can the other fellow know we know it? This yes-and-no manner of thinking was troublesome. For example, did I love you? *Yes* because you were so much like me, and *no* because I was going to harm you. But perhaps this "no" was merely a confirmation of the "yes"? Even as I was thinking you began to talk.

"You're the poetry-lover," you said, "and I'm the one who is embarrassed by poetry, but even so there are exceptions. There are poets who don't embarrass me—a very few. I think that's because the content of what they have written is as good as the rhyme and the meter. Usually, poetry is all meter and no sense. Do you know the one about 'sin of self-love'?"

"What makes you remember that just now?" I asked, for that you were thinking along the same lines as I was only another corroboration that you were coming too close to robbing me of my integrity and individuality. I would have to hurry with my plans.

"Oh, I don't know," you replied carelessly. "I like your Shakespearean sonnets. They fit in everywhere; like jewels, equally beautiful in the bathtub or at the Royal Ball."

"''Tis thee, myself—that for myself I praise,'" I quoted.

"I wonder what he meant," you mused, frowning, taking your hand from mine and placing it again on the wheel. "Does he mean we love ourselves most, or does he mean when we love another we love only what we see reflected there of ourselves?"

"That would contradict the opposites-attract argument," I inserted.

"A poor argument anyway. Does the lion attract the lamb? Or the sun the rain?"

"But man attracts woman," I pointed out.

"Man and woman aren't opposites," you said, surprised. "They are the same." You drove in silence, and then laughed and quoted, "'Methinks no face so gracious is as mine, No shape so true, no truth of such account; And for myself mine own worth do define, As I all other in all worths surmount.' What's your worth?" you asked, glancing quickly at me.

"To myself," I told you, drawing on my gloves as we neared the little park in the center of town where you would drop me, "to myself I'm worth the world. 'And for this sin there is no remedy.' Here, this is my corner. Let me out."

As you slowed the car to a stop by the curb of a small park, a ragged urchin sped out from the fountains where he had been wading and held the door open for me in the hope of earning a small tip.

"Listen," you said, giving the child a coin, as I gathered up my hat and my bag. "Listen. About this afternoon. It didn't happen. None of it was true." You spoke clipped and hurriedly.

"I know," I answered gently, and slipped out of the car.

No chronicling of a relationship can be complete without a reference to the letters which invariably are exchanged over a period of years. Letters are as much a part of love-making as kisses, and you and I wrote to each other such a variety as would make a separate book.

There were the letters we exchanged about business matters on those occasions when you took your yearly two weeks' vacation, or when I accepted invitations in the country on the ranches of friends, or travelled, as seldom as possible, with the old lawyer and his multitude of cigars, to another city for a convention or to charm a political client in order to increase the power and prestige of the firm.

Then there were the notes; mine neatly written on pale-blue embossed stationery, yours hurriedly scribbled on the nearest bit of paper and squashed into any old envelope, notes confirming engagements, notes to thank for gifts, notes calling books or magazine articles to each other's attention, notes containing passages from books, or quotations or some point won in an argument, notes acknowledging payments of debts, flurries and hail of notes.

The actual personal letters exchanged between us were

few and these unusual. I remember the Holy Week holidays when you awarded yourself a weekend at the beginning and end of the vacation and flew to a northern resort for mountain climbing in the mild almost summery weather. You had once told me that whoever of us went from the other must do the lion's share of writing, for it was always most difficult to stay behind. You were good about long-distance telephone calls, postal cards and telegrams, but you liked to avoid writing letters, they committed you too deeply and you looked upon being committed as if it were a peculiar and horrible disease instead of being a pleasant and lucrative attachment.

The Holy Week letter from you that particular year stands out in my memory because of the disappointment that followed it. I had not really expected you to write in a ten days' absence, and when your first short letter came I was pleased; you were as good as your word. It was more of a note than a letter, resuming an interrupted conversation by adding the concluding phrases, nothing more. When you telephoned me I was certain that I would not receive another letter from you. How could I suspect you would once be honest enough to rush from the telephone to the writing-desk and tell me on paper what you could not bring yourself to say? Such spontaneity was most foreign to you.

When your second Holy Week letter came I thought it must contain business documents, for it lay, bulky and important, on my breakfast-tray as out of place with the dainty porcelain as it could be. I opened it without much interest, expecting you had sent me a copy of some report tardily executed, or photostats taken along by mistake, anything indeed that pertained to business. I remember shaking the sheets out and watching them scatter over my bed as I realized you had written me a long hand-penned affair, twelve, fourteen, sixteen pages of your writing, all of it personal.

I played with the letter before reading it, such an unlooked-for luxury was too delicious to be swallowed hastily. Here and there I caught glimpses of words, bits of sentences, and still I toyed with the airmail sheets and the gaudy envelope, examining your writing, the contours of your letters, pretending I did not know you and endeavoring to determine your character from your penmanship, reading your handwriting instead of your words.

It would be foolish to claim you had written a masterpiece. You had done nothing of the sort. Your letter was impetuous and revealing, your grammar abominable and your sentiments all I could wish for. You tried incoherently enough to describe the mountains to me and ended up by describing how you felt walking in them without me. You attempted to tell me tidbits about the guests, but they bored you, for without me in the hotel everyone seemed dull. You sent me your love, your longing; you refused to admit you would much rather have stayed behind with me, but that confession was implicit in every line. You talked of the sunset, you who never allowed the faintest breath of mush to color your relationship to me, and, worse, you wrote of the moon! The moon had obviously aroused all your latent sex and you bayed like a dog at it, in writing of course, and properly addressed to the proper source. Still, you spent paragraphs on the moon. There was no mention of the sweet scent of flowers so I presumed the roses were missing and I doubted you could recognize any other flower.

My elation over this lengthy exposition of your want for me was as absurd as the letter itself. I was giddy with satisfaction, I felt like a young girl and I knew whoever saw me that day would know I loved and was loved, for the pleasure of it had spread all through my body and face and I could feel myself glowing with life and vigor and power. You wrote you loved me and I had never hoped to see that in writing, I could hardly elicit the words from you in whispers let alone obtain them for re-examination whenever I chose to read the bit of paper where you had written them. For once you had not obliged me to read between the lines, for once you had forsaken all trickery, for once I could read through every page with pleasure, over and over again; you loved me, yet more love and greater desire, less restraint, increased passion. I fell into an ecstasy and dawdled the morning away in bed with your letter. I calculated it must have taken you all night to write it to me and you must have posted it in the early morning, around dawn. I was pleased almost to tears with your youthfulness.

Although at that time I knew you well, I still did not know you well enough. In the afternoon I received a telephone call from the novia which surprised me; she rarely called me. It seemed she was on her way to a club dance in my neighborhood and wanted to drop in to pay her respects in your absence. I knew that something was in the wind, but lulled by the security of your letter, I was rashly prepared to face anything.

The novia came just as I was walking out on the terrace to reread your letter over solitary cocktails in the *heure bleue* of early evening. She wore a long dancing-dress and a fur wap which I suspected she had borrowed for pure show as the evening was warm. I realized she had come for a purpose which must, in some way, be connected with you, but I hardly cared what it might be. She accepted a cocktail and stretched out in one of the garden lounges, carefully arranging her dress with a spinsterish finicketyness to avoid unnecessary creases. I had pushed your letter into my bag and flung the bag where I could see the bulge the letter made in its beaded side.

We chatted politely; yes, she had hoped to attend the dance with you but as you needed a vacation so badly (poor boy you were working so hard, she claimed) she had sent you off (a lie, I knew) and she was being escorted by somebody else, but he would call for her at the house, my house, wouldn't come in to bother me, but in a half hour or so . . . I was not curious and the bait did not tempt me.

The novia hedged a bit more, commenting on the unusual warmth of the evening, how pretty the fireflies looked in the garden, what a lovely shade my gown was. When I was least prepared for it, she brought it out.

"Can you imagine?" she said shrilly. "The impossible has happened! He actually has written me a letter, a long letter!"

While I watched, her nervous fingers fumbled in her handbag and she brought out a heavy, bulky envelope, identical to mine in size and shape, your handwriting sprawled over its face. I would willingly have burst into tears had it been possible to do so. I could feel my vigor seeping out of me, through my toes and chin so that my face dropped; I was thankful for the fading light which could not reveal how telling a blow the novia had struck.

"Well, my dear," I returned smoothly, "I'm sure you must get many letters. It's a habit of young men to write to the girls they're in love with!" I could not bring myself to say "the girls they love."

"But he never writes!" the novia cried out. "Not to anybody. He's afraid he might commit himself!" She did not see me wince and babbled on. "He sends you his best; here, I'll read it to you, that's really why I came." She was unfolding the stiff sheets, thumbing through them, muttering to herself. "Ah, here it is; 'and say that I am looking forward to sitting again on the terrace and having a quiet drink and am quite ready to go back to work. Vacations are necessary but overrated, one is really happiest when one is with the people one belongs to.'" Here the novia gave me a triumphant look. "It goes on again, more about you," she observed, "but I can't find it, it's in the back somewhere."

In the poor, deceptive light my eyes could not distinguish the words you had written her although there they were, a few tantalising feet from me.

"Oh, never mind, my dear," I said carelessly, "I'm sure your young man wants to be polite to me and I'm equally sure he is." I hoped I did not sound too sour. "Ah, here's the butler, no doubt your tonight's young man is at the door.

What a gay life you lead! How I envy you!" I went on lightly, rising as the novia rose.

"You?" the novia exclaimed rather than asked, facing me. "You envy me? You couldn't envy anybody! You have everything!"

"How nice of you to say so!" I told her, wanting to slap her for the unconscious irony of her praise.

When she left, I ran to the vestibule to catch a glimpse of the young man who had come to call for her. I thought I saw a shock of blond hair but I wasn't sure; it might have been the moonlight glinting on a carefully brushed young male head.

Returned, in the dark, to the terrace, I watched the butler light the candles in their glass wind-protectors and then, when I was again alone, I tore up, without rereading, your romantic and impassioned letter, slowly and deliberately, and dropped the tiny pieces into the candle to be consumed by the small flame. You had beggared me and so now I burned you in effigy.

That was, unfortunately, the only love-letter you ever wrote me.

CHAPTER NINE 🖋

As a well-known widow,
running a big house, entertaining a good deal, busy with
charities, retaining a fairly active interest in the law-firm and
ranch left to me by my second husband, I had found it easiest to live according to a set program, reserving specific days
in the week for consultations with the various heads of charities, with the foreman reporting on the proceeds or deficits
of the farm, with different members of the numerous
branches of the business. I entertained exclusively over week-

ends; every Wednesday I went to town for shopping and whatever unavoidable engagements I might have incurred. People who knew me were aware of this program; I so rarely varied it that even when I did nobody took note of it.

When I discovered I was gaining weight despite the swimming and desultory tennis I engaged in, I resolved to take hard exercise without making an exhibition of myself. My vanity did not want to be exposed to any comments; I was proud of my body. For a woman of over forty it was excellent; women fully ten years my junior envied me my figure and I had no intention of losing it, least of all at this time. I took up bicycling as a reducing sport, pedalling about the less frequented suburban paths at an hour when almost nobody was ever to be met on the streets, the inviolable siesta hour, three to four. I did this exercise without joy and mentioned it to nobody.

On these bicycle rides I met the milkmen going about their afternoon deliveries, or the horse-carts of the grocery stores, a few beggars lounging in doorways pleading for food, and a host of stray dogs and cats. With the exception of a fat, deaf woman who used to wave at me as I wheeled by (I had no idea who she was, only that she apparently spent the day knitting on her veranda and my going by was a friendly event) I met no one and greeted no one.

When the weather was especially hot I usually stopped off at an inn for a glass of cold orange-juice; nobody was ever in the inn gardens and I had adopted the practice of walking directly to the kitchen door to order and drink my orange-juice, skirting the deserted gardens entirely. In brief, I took this exercise in secret, nobody ever suspected me of it, and I retained a firm, well-proportioned body with no superfluity of fat and no necessity of corsets.

Some ten days after your talk with me about marrying the novia, I was pedalling under a hot sun towards the inn which I had come to regard as the half-way point in my hour's marathon. There was no thought in my head except cold orange-juice. My immediate goal was the attainment of that glass, and I biked with my head lowered, the sweat pouring down my back between my shoulder blades. The image of the glass of fruit-juice was before my eyes as I toiled up the last hill to the inn without diminishing my speed. I turned the corner to the inn's delivery entrance and then braked suddenly. Parked before the main gates, twenty yards up the street, was a long, low open car which I recognized at once as the stooge's. It was clean and shining, an unmistakable pleasure car; nobody was in it.

I cycled up the delivery entrance quickly, not troubling to look into the gardens but noticing out of the corner of my eye that two people sat at one of the small tables under a parasol. From the kitchen, as I drank my orange-juice and talked with the cook about the hot weather, I could look out over the gardens through a small window. Usually, I stood in the doorway as I drank, the better to keep an eye on my bicycle, but this time I edged to the window and peered out.

The stooge, his blond head bent towards her, was talking earnestly to the novia. His hand, on the table, covered hers and he shook her wrist as he spoke. In his free hand he held a cigarette; I saw the slow smoke curl upwards as he held it away from her, below the table.

Paying for my orange-juice, I decided to cycle out around the block and approach the inn again from the opposite side. I could stand behind the hedge which backed the table with the parasol and hear, without difficulty, what these two were saying to each other. It was my first intimation that the stooge and the novia knew each other. I thought you had kept them apart.

Executing my plan I cycled silently to a standstill under a tree beside the dense hedge. Their voices came to me clearly through the foliage.

"Darling, darling," the stooge was saying, "what on earth are you hesitating for? You've only got one life to live."

He had a deep voice, rather pleasant, and now it flowed out to the novia in a passion of persuasion.

"I know. But there are so many factors to consider." As always, when the novia was excited, her voice tended to become a bit shrill.

"None of the factors count except that I love you and you love me," the stooge assured her in a positive tone; and then as she made no answer he asked, almost plaintively, "You *do* love me, don't you, sweetheart?"

In the long interval before the novia's reply I heard the locusts start up their metallic, penetrating heat-song and the air was noisy with their screaming. I dared not part the crisp leaves of the hedge to peer at the couple for fear the crackling of the dry branches might reveal my presence and I was obliged to content myself with imagining how they looked at each other, what positions they adopted on the hard iron chairs, what caresses and breathings they demonstrated.

"Of course I love you," the novia said at last, in a rush. "But there's more to marriage than just love!"

I was surprised at this practical streak in the novia before such a romantic proposition. I doubted she would have made such an observation had you, instead of the stooge, been sitting beside her.

"Well, we have all the money in the world, tons more than we could ever spend," the stooge told her with a touch of pride. "What more can one have?"

Oh, I thought angrily, leaning on the handlebars of my bicycle, the stupidity of the younger generation, forever talking of money as if it were possible to buy anything with it: love, friendship, loyalty, interest. Admittedly, money went a long way to securing the *semblance* of these things, but if one chose to believe in such abstracts (and so make them real) money would not purchase them.

"And then," the novia said hesitantly, "I wouldn't want to hurt anyone."

I nearly laughed aloud at this. There was a long silence during which we three, they on one side of the hedge, and I on the other, thought of you. How could the novia hope to deceive the stooge with such a story, I wondered. Surely, if the stooge were as close a friend of yours as you claimed he was, he must know it was not possible for anyone to hurt you, except (although this he could *not* know) myself. A woman as insecure and bewildered and frankly abused by you as the novia, had no power to hurt you, and you would never permit your "friend," this paragon of perfection that was the stooge, to hurt you. You were untouchable, invincible to everyone save me.

"Has he asked you to marry him?" the stooge inquired finally, his young voice deeper than before.

"Yes."

I didn't doubt the truth of this; I could imagine you saying casually, after a dance or a theatre, "Come on, let's take the night-boat and cross the river and get married." And when the novia agreed you had probably said, "Fine, let's make it a week from Thursday, give me time to get a licence; and you better buy a black nightgown or something." And then a week from Thursday you probably telephoned and told her you had an engagement to take me to the theatre or a concert or to drive me to somebody's house. I suspect you had played cat-and-mouse with the novia on the marriage issue so often that she had eventually come to realize you were not really serious about it. You simply enjoyed the knowledge that you could marry her if you wanted to.

"Well, why didn't you marry him, then?" the stooge asked roughly.

"Oh, darling," the novia cried out, "don't be so sensitive!"

"But I want to know," the stooge persisted, unmollified. "Was it because of me that you didn't accept him?"

Eternal male vanity, I commented to myself. Or had the stooge become contaminated by your vanity? My damp hands slipped along the chromium handlebars and the front wheel of my bicycle slithered suddenly about. I was afraid the noise might distract the couple, but they were concen-

could see me, be cowed by my look and retract his statement. My eyes met only the gentle green front of the hedge. On the other hand, I thought rapidly, wasn't this observation, or, better said, this summary of me exactly what I wanted people to think? Should anyone know that I had my passions and weaknesses and unconquerable desires and, worse still, that I gratified them with you? Wasn't it the most human action in the world to preserve one's life, and wasn't that precisely what I was doing, at your expense, of course, but when one is attacked as you had attacked my personality, my woman-hood, wasn't it inevitable, as in any medieval contest be-tween two knights of equal or almost equal strengths that one of the contestants should perish? Wasn't it human to wish that the contestant who perished would be the other fellow and not oneself? Wasn't I observing the first law of being human, the law of maintaining myself?

"I certainly was no match for the widow," the novia re-marked gloomily, and I could imagine her sitting dejectedly in the chair. "I've been brought up wrong. All the books say that a girl of twenty wins out against a woman of forty. The freshness of youth and all that. But no books ever tell you what an unconquerable enemy a well-preserved woman of forty really is!"

I frowned at the novia, glaring at the hedge. I disliked that "well-preserved."

"Is she really forty?" the stooge asked with interest.

His question caused me to smile. Men always thought bet-ter of me than women were apt to. Not that men were more charitable, they were merely less discerning.

"Probably much more," the novia replied bitingly; "if she confesses to forty, you can be sure she's well over."

"Are you sure," the stooge asked after a short, meditative pause, "that you don't still love him? Maybe I'm just getting you on the rebound?"

"Does it matter how you're getting me?" the novia demanded, and I heard the tears in her voice. "I'm through with him! No girl can stand a man who's forever comparing her to a goddess. I admit I'm made of clay! Why must I be scolded for it? And anyway, darling," she went on in an altered voice with more talent for theatre than I had given her credit for, "anyway, if I hadn't known him, I'd never have met you."

"Well, we're back to the widow," the stooge observed with a sigh. "Because *she* introduced him to you."

"Oh, let's not talk about the widow!" the novia begged. "Let's talk about us."

Yes, I commented slyly to myself, now we will have the castles-in-Spain which will probably turn out to resemble my own house and way of life, for no doubt you had educated the novia to appreciate the things it had taken me years to learn to value.

"There's only one thing to talk about," the stooge answered. "When shall we get married?"

Marriage, marriage, I thought disgustedly. How the male animal rushes to embrace monogamy, and a few years later is rushing away from it, all out for polygamy or harems.

"Give me a little time, darling," the novia pleaded, "to straighten myself out. And I have to tell him, of course. He'll be hurt because he's taken me so completely for granted. After all, I'm almost the widow's creation; he told me so himself. The widow gave me to him, he said. He's so in love with her that every other woman is just a poor reflection of her!"

In the distance I heard the approach of horse's hooves, the slow clatter-clatter of the milkman's tired mare on her way to the stable. Should I permit myself to be seen, so obviously eavesdropping? I began assiduously to fuss with my shoes and remained bent over until the horse and cart had passed me. I was afraid the milkman might make some comment or even offer to help me, but the heat of the afternoon had dulled him as completely as his nag, and the episode passed successfully.

"Everything *does* seem to revolve around her, doesn't it?" the novia said after the brief silence.

"I know one thing that won't revolve around her," the stooge snapped out grimly. "And that's our honeymoon. Suppose we talk about it? After all, that'll be our first long time together, when we'll start to know each other. I mean, I mean," he floundered, "the honeymoon is important. It sets the pitch for the rest. You know. Where would you like to go?" His voice became more authoritative as he fell on firmer ground. "I know thousands of lovely places."

"Honeymoon?" the novia echoed vaguely and with a little touch of fright in her voice. "Oh, darling, I don't know. Let's go some place clean and sunny."

"How about skiing?" the stooge suggested eagerly. "Lots of snow and sun."

"But I don't know how to ski," the novia protested.

"I'll teach you," the stooge offered happily. "You'll love it. Just us together in the woods with the snow. You have no idea how wonderful it will be."

Such a prospect appealed even to me considering the wretched heat of the day. I saw the inviting slopes of shallow hills, snow-covered, before me, glistening in the sun. I wondered if I could learn to ski or if perhaps I was not already too old and stiff.

"I wonder if the widow skis?" the novia speculated ruminatively.

"Damn the widow!" the stooge shouted. "Get her out of your mind! I don't want to live with the woman!" He called for the waiter and, still shouting at the novia, went on, "We're going for a long drive in the country and we'll leave the widow out there to hell and gone and I don't want to hear about her again!"

Hearing them rise from the table, I quickly turned my bicycle about, mounted hurriedly, and pedalled rapidly away. Although I heard the noise of their motor starting up in the still afternoon I knew they would not come in my direction and did not trouble to leave the main road. They roared around the corner and disappeared in the opposite distance. The perfect woman, I thought bitterly, biking in secret to keep her weight down in order to be attractive to a younger man. What folly, what uncondonable folly.

The following week, in order to determine if the novia actually had told you of her coming marriage to your best friend, the stooge, I invited you and her to a birthday dinner

I was giving for my old lawyer. When you entered the drawing-room together for cocktails I was strongly tempted to provoke a dramatic scene with the novia. I needed only to look at her to see how deeply in love with you she was and how difficult she was going to find it to be through with you. Obviously she had told you nothing; she stayed close to you with an almost pathetic, dog-like devotion. I noticed, then, for the first time, how frequently you looked at me. Love, I thought angrily, is most certainly public property; it cannot be concealed.

I longed to make a reference to the novia about her talk with the stooge in the tea house, and the desire to behave detestably struggled against my good manners. I kept away from her, not trusting myself to be near her; at dinner I placed her next to a newspaperman who I thought might help her in her career if she planned to continue working while married. After the speeches and birthday toasts we gathered in the music-room to hear a new quintet I had bought and whatever other records anyone might choose. I hung back a moment in the drawing-room to arrange some ashtrays and adjust a misplaced porcelain figure; as a consequence I was the last to enter the room.

In that instant that I crossed the threshold I had a positive and strong feeling that something was going to happen to me. I thought this feeling had to do with your novia and I looked sharply at her, but she was talking animatedly to the newspaperman, ostensibly happy. Looking at you, I found your back turned towards me; you were politely lighting somebody's cigarette.

CHAPTER TEN 🖋

The windows were open and I seated myself on the window-seat, partly for the breeze, partly to be near the gramophone and change the records. Leaving the lady with her cigarette, you perched on a bar-stool at the opposite end of the room, facing me, leaning with your back against the bar itself. The novia took a stool around the curve of the bar, behind you but unable to see me because of a larger, white Chinese lamp that obstructed her view.

The other guests had settled on the sofa and in various chairs and relaxed, stirring hot black coffee, sniffing into the bellied brandy glasses, digesting contentedly like so many over-fed animals in a particularly well-appointed zoo. Out of this atmosphere of gross well-being somebody suggested we save the quintet for later and play the Beethoven Ninth Symphony now. I did not know who had spoken, it had been a woman's voice, but not the novia's; most likely your lady of the cigarette anxious to impress you with her excellent taste in music. There were murmurs of appreciation. That request was a corroboration in itself of my presentment that the evening would be unusual. And yet, I thought, as I took the album from its shelf and placed the discs on the gramophone, what could happen? You and I were six meters apart in a roomful of people; what conceivable contact could we have in the presence of your novia, my lawyer and an assortment of guests? There were no hidden corners in the room, the soft glow of various lamps shed an almost even light everywhere. Why, exactly, had the Ninth Symphony been asked for? There were eight others, four of which were indubitably more popular.

Even as I pressed the button to start the symphony, I knew that whatever was going to happen would happen with the playing of the third movement, for that movement had been one of the best-liked bits of music of my dead husband. The gramophone was to be dignified with the role of catalyst in an unknown precipitation, and I was apprehensive as well as curious.

I changed the records carefully and quietly; somebody

commented on the first movement. Your novia, I could see, had taken to smoking (a sure indication of uneasiness); you sat in exactly the same position at the bar; two of the ladies were talking sotto voce together, comparing recipes or servant trouble I surmised; one gentleman frankly had fallen asleep; the remainder of the company listened gravely to the music. There was nothing unusual in the room or in the people; the music itself, for all the expectancy it contains, was familiar, almost reassuring. The dogs barked in the garden, the wind sniffled lightly in the eucalyptus trees, the music rolled out for almost five uninterrupted minutes with each record. At the conclusion of the second movement, the man who had been asleep awakened, looked about sheepishly and whispered across to me to know what was being played. I placed the needle in its groove on the record and the first part of the third movement filled the room.

And suddenly I heard, beyond the music, the humming noise that I had experienced with you before, only this time very high and mosquito-thin and I found that you and I were talking together but *in silence,* without moving our lips, without even looking at each other. I could hear you, as you spoke to me, as clearly and convincingly as if you had stood next to me and conversed close to my ear.

Love scenes usually take place in private and with all the intimacy of caress and compliment. Ours took place then, in public, with nobody aware of us. Why on that particular evening the erotic, which is at the basis of every relationship between the sexes, should have reached its greatest height I do not attempt to explain. But at no time before, not even when I had lain in your arms, had I felt so *pulled* towards you as during this part of the evening.

It began when I found I was standing by the piano in exactly the same position in which I had stood the evening I had kissed the palm of your hand. Unthinkingly, I looked over at the record shelves and sought out the titles of the pieces we had played at that time, especially the Bach. Then I consulted you to see if you were also remembering, and our glances met as you turned your attention from a study of the record shelves to me. Although you had not changed your position on the barstool, your hands had assumed an odd relaxation. Only after a few seconds did I discover your left palm was turned upwards and two fingertips of your right hand pressed in its center as if pointing out *here, here*. Were you aware of this gesture? I looked away, staring at the white Chinese lamp, and your voice came to me so smoothly and naturally that I found myself replying to you without quite grasping that our conversation was conducted in silence and that we were engaged in an extraordinary adventure.

"Very well," you were saying to me. "I give up the struggle. You have won. Are you satisfied?"

"Satisfied?" I repeated. "I don't honestly know."

"There's nothing more to have or to want," you went on. "Shall we run away now to the South Seas or wherever you like and spend the rest of our lives reading each other's thoughts?"

"I'm not reading your thoughts. I'm talking with myself. We all talk with ourselves," I protested.

"Shall I write down what we're saying?" you asked me and, as I jerked up my head to look at you across the room I met your eyes and watched you take out of your pocket a small notebook, the sort of thing in which one keeps one's engagements, and a thin silver pencil. "You are afraid," you told me. "With all your scheming and planning you didn't foresee this. You have never been able to read anyone else's thoughts, have you? You have never known what it means to *be* the other fellow, to lose your identity? You have never known anything at all about real possession, have you, as you are possessing me now? You have never loved so deeply that there no longer is any difference between you and the subject of your love, have you?" The pencil had not moved, however, and I clung to it as a sign that possibly we were not talking to each other, possibly I was really talking only with myself. "I shall write down your answer," I heard you say.

"I don't want to lose my identity! I don't want to be you!" I cried out within myself and I saw your pencil begin to move, writing rapidly in the notebook.

"If you don't want to be me, you don't love me," I heard you say. Your voice went on, through the music, almost as if it came out of the music. "You are shocked that I, instead of you, have some talents, have the same sensitivity you have, that *I* can force you to have a relationship with me, that *I* can reach you as completely as . . ."

The music stopped and so did your voice. I changed the record hurriedly and immediately your voice went on.

". . . as I am doing. I don't request a surrender. *I* surrender. What more can you ask?"

"I haven't thought, I haven't thought," I replied, and I saw you write again in the notebook and then underline what you had written. That underlining, I understood at once, was a sign for "repeat."

"Yes, of course I love you, I want you. What more do you want to hear? Love, love, love. Or is it possible you don't know what to do with me once you have me? Are you only a fighter and a destroyer, you who think so much about love? Or are you also a lover?"

"I'm not a lover," I answered. "Women are never lovers. We are destroyers if we are strong, and if we are weak we are able to do no more than contort. We pretend to love. How else shall we have a chance to destroy? We can't survive unless we destroy what we love."

"Will you destroy me?"

"I am trying to," I answered.

"Because you love me?"

"Because I love you," I admitted.

"Wouldn't it be easier for you to destroy me if you came and lived with me? Anywhere in the world, anywhere you please?"

Nobody was watching us, I noticed in a hurried glance about the room, so I dared to look into your eyes.

"I can't destroy you if I live with you," I answered.

"So you have a weak spot, an Achilles' heel. The beloved is not invincible. You know you will be destroyed by me if you live with me. What a slow and tender and lovely destruction. A disintegration through love. Aren't you tempted?"

"I am not tempted!" I shouted and clapped my hand over my mouth, prepared that everybody in the room jump, startled, to his feet and ask for explanations. Nobody moved. I had not uttered a sound.

"Each of us in this world wants to be loved, loved as much as we love ourselves. Since we are each other, you and I, that is the way I love you. More love is impossible."

"You are not me!" I contradicted. "We are separate. I will not be yours!"

"This is no question of will. It is an identification of two beings. Lovers are always saying they wish to be one and clutching each other in bed to try to make it so. We are one, across the room, for we are identical. Come and live with yourself, called by my name, in my body. Don't you want to live with yourself if I am you? I want to live with myself since I am you. I ache to live with you. Do you know what it is to ache with desire? Stop making a face as if you are about to cry!"

I looked quickly past your shoulder into the mirror above the bar and, rightly enough, my face was puckered up, I was chewing at my underlip and I appeared as if in a tantrum. The music stopped and I knew I must turn the record for the second half of the movement but I could not move. Suddenly the novia's voice rang across the room asking me if I would like her to change the records, it was such a nuisance. Both you and I looked at her and I could feel we wore the same expressions of astonishment on our faces. No sooner had I turned the record and the music continued when your voice said to me:

"You see, we had both completely forgotten about her and we jumped like old women when she spoke!"

This queer talk had lasted already a little over ten minutes and I was becoming used to it. Even the strangest happenings, upon prolongation, become accepted as usual.

"You are not to think," your voice said, "that we will talk like this again. We never will."

"How do you know?" I asked, and couldn't help adding, "How theatrical that sounds, *we never will.*"

A hint of a smile came to your mouth at variance with the tender singing of the music.

"It will never again be exactly like this between us, and only when it's exactly like this can we talk."

"So you admit there is no such thing as repetition!" I exclaimed triumphantly.

Across the room, your mouth hidden now by your hand in your usual gesture, you nodded your head at me.

"We are losing time," you reprimanded. "I am asking you to live with me."

"I don't dare," I said flatly.

"The beloved is becoming insecure; first she is vulnerable and now she is cowardly."

"Insults don't matter, even if justified. Under no condition can I come," I told you, and was afraid to think further because you would read my added thought.

"But the beloved would like to live with me."

There was still one record to play before the movement

174

drew to a close and I wondered how I should come through it. To be offered a love that one desires and to refuse it in order to live, to retain one's individuality, is a very difficult denial. I decided to render myself immune to any additional temptation by concentrating on the worst offence you had ever given me. It was an episode I had never wholly forgotten nor forgiven and I resurrected it as I settled the needle in the groove. Immediately I heard your voice.

"Don't think of that," you urged. "I apologize for it. That's what you've been waiting for me to do, isn't it? I'm ashamed of it. Stop thinking of it!"

I ignored your appeal and carefully began to reconstruct the offence down to its smallest detail.

You had asked me, the previous year, to meet you in your flat for cocktails; after that I had to attend a dull dinner party. As it happened, the dinner party was cancelled, which I told you, and as a consequence you postponed our cocktail date to a much later hour, the ordinary dinner hour of the town, and I presumed we would dine together. We had cocktails in your flat, and, after half an hour, you stood up and said you were sorry but you had to leave me to go to *your* dinner engagement.

I made my displeasure very clear; it was only when I learned you were off to the novia's house for dinner that I understood what you had tried to do. You were trying to hurt me by inflicting an insult upon me; you dared to leave me for the more tempting joys the novia had to offer; it was your supreme effort to make me jealous, to show me you were neither afraid of me nor very interested in me. As

175

such, it turned into a fiasco. I said I would remain in your flat to finish my drink at my leisure and you had a bad moment wondering how much of your private papers I might read in your absence. I forestalled your worry by telling you I had, at my age, read so many private papers that their contents could no longer arouse my curiosity. You left bearishly, refusing to kiss me, utterly disgruntled with yourself. Your evening with the novia was spoiled in any case.

I sat, half reclined, on the sofa and reflected. When a man deliberately endeavors to hurt a woman he desires it is only because he has begun to resent her power over him. You had planned this offence, for offence it most certainly was, against both good manners and affection, and, of course, I understood you wanted a certain reaction from me out of it. You wanted, I analysed thoughtfully, a long and passionate letter, a pained but well-written cry of anguish. This would give *you* a pleasant sense of power over *me,* a delightful reversal of our roles. You would not have minded had I torn your clothes, destroyed your papers, thrown your books on the floor and broken your furniture, for such an outburst would have been a gratifying indication of how deeply you had wounded me and how unable I had been to control myself. Or, best of all, you hoped to find me on your return waiting for you, sad-eyed and wretched. In your place, any of these alternatives would have appealed to me, too.

What, then, did you *least* expect from a woman you had treated badly? Whatever that was, that would constitute my weapon. It slipped into my mind easily, a ready-made answer, completely obvious: *humor.* That a woman could have, in the outrageous situation of being abandoned by her lover (for that's what it amounted to in miniature) a sense of humor would be a hard blow for you. What could I do that would be humorous?

There was still a glassful of Martini in the shaker and I poured it reflectively, sipped it slowly and examined the humorous possibilities of your apartment. I could risk nothing that would conceivably fall flat. I consulted the pictures and bric-à-brac and books for inspiration, and I am indebted to a paper-bound French novel one of your flirts had given you for the idea that came to me. I did not find what I needed in your living-room so I penetrated to your bedroom and there, on your dresser, I found one of those round, inviting, rather deep ashtrays that are used the world over in ladies' public lavatories; the kind of receptacle that always holds fifty or sixty cents as a sign to the next customer that, for the use of plumbing, towel and soap, she is expected to swell the offerings to whatever fat and sexless creature presides over those high-class urinals. Emerging from your bathroom, I had left this ashtray on the only seat of the hygienic room, with twenty cents clanking about inside it. Satisfied, I left your apartment, smiling at the use I had made of it.

"I had wanted a letter, of course," your voice assured me. "But I hadn't really expected one." The music was drawing to a close. "Are you going to evade a lifetime with me because of that scene?" your voice persisted. "Does it really come down to the two hours I should have but didn't spend with you? For that you will let everything slip by?"

"I am letting nothing slip by," I assured you, watching the

arm of the gramophone travel nearer and nearer to the shining smooth black center of the record where the music would end.

"Nothing, everything; we have no idea what the words mean. Leave words alone and come to me now, quickly, across the room before the music ends. We are deciding our future. Come, come now."

"One of us," I began grimly, and then the music closed and, although I finished my sentence, I knew you could not hear it, "is not going to have a future."

I put the records away in the album, noticing that the high humming, which had accompanied your voice, had also disappeared. My ears seemed to be filled with a great emptiness, almost as if I were deaf. I drifted towards the bar. Your novia was talking with the old lawyer; your notebook lay open on the counter. I looked curiously at you, afraid the talk might continue and the really irresistible temptation to fling myself at you and melt into you would revive. Instead, after the astonishing intimacy of our dialogue, we seemed to be strangers. I began to doubt that the talk had taken place; your eyes were cloudy, in the familiar signal of desire, but speculative and even a bit remote. Your hand covered your mouth.

I reached for the notebook fully expecting to see nothing but blank pages, happy in anticipating my own relief at being able to say:

"It was all imagined, nothing happened, I ate too much suckling pig at dinner and had an halucination."

The two pages of the tiny book were untidily scribbled

over; you had not noted all that we had said, only scraps, but these scraps were ample proof for me. I read: *I don't want to be you. I haven't thought. I am not tempted! One of us . . .*

I considered confiscating the notebook in order to refer to it the following day when I could reflect in quiet on what had taken place, but you forestalled me by taking it out of my hands, wordlessly, and slipping it into your pocket. I could not very well ask you, before others, for your own engagement book.

And yet, what had taken place, was it then so very odd? How many times in our lives have we not said to the other fellow, "I bet I know what you're thinking!" and how many times have we not been quite correct in our guesses. Where is the line between guessing and feeling and knowing?

And had this scene not had its antecedent, its preparative, as it were? I had but to think back to the university and there I saw the groundwork laid for just this experience.

It had been a warm Saturday afternoon and, coming out of the college library, I had had the luck to run into her. She was dressed in a strawberry-colored shirt and dark-green skirt and I remember thinking what an unusual color-combination this was. I had not let my chance slip by but at once accosted her with the conventional salutation.

"Hello! What are you up to? Not going to grind *now,* are you?"

"I was going for a walk," she had said, and the lameness and unoriginality of this proclaimed its truth. Her eyes met mine fleetingly and then slipped away to watch other stu-

dents coming out of the libe, to examine the bicycles standing in their wooden racks, to look at the fat robins on the
lawn.

"That's a good idea," I had observed. "Mind if I join you?"

"No, no, of course not. I mean, do." She had been so utterly confused and had not known in which direction to turn
to initiate the walk.

"Shall we climb the hill behind the golf course?" I had
suggested, "and sit on top in the apple orchard and look
down on everyone?"

She had consulted her wristwatch and frowned.

"But there isn't time, is there?" she had protested timidly.
"I mean, before supper?"

"Let's forget supper."

We had started out together solemnly, crossing the campus like any two ordinary students, each of us actually in a
frenzy of anticipation. Late golfers were coming down the
fairways; the course had stretched before us, sparsely dotted
with a few hurrying players rushing through the last two
holes. The hill sloped slowly upwards to the apple orchard
that graced its summit; we had begun to climb, concentratedly and carefully, but rapidly. I had led the way to a
fallen tree trunk on the brow of the hill and had sat down
in the long grass with my back resting against it. The campus with its many grey Gothic buildings had sprawled before me, academic, distant and very much like a picture
postcard. She had had to sit next to me; where else on the
hill could she have sat?

The sun had lowered beyond the thin spires of the music

building; we had heard the clang of the gongs in the various dormitories announcing supper; a light wind had sprung up from the distant river and ruffled through the orchard behind us. A fine calm had descended with the evening; the intellects babbled over their supper, filling their expensive stomachs, and we two heretics lounged on the hilltop and enjoyed, guiltily, our apartness.

Does anything bring two people closer together than the sensation that they are different from their fellows? I had leaned on my elbow in an easy Roman attitude and my head had just touched her shoulder, a natural student's posture, casual, nothing that would ever have caused a second glance, nothing in any way scandalous and yet such a significant and intimate contact to both of us that we might as well have been nude. We were so completely attuned to each other that any move the one might have made would have been wordlessly and thankfully accepted by the other, but we were young and lacking in both experience and courage and so we sat quietly side by side instead of executing the passionate embraces and kisses that we were each imagining. And we had known we were both thinking the same thing, each madly desiring the other, for my head had rested firmer against her shoulder and she had shifted her position the better to accommodate it. Even when she had looked down at me and I had had but to raise my face to receive her kiss, convention and shyness interfered and I pulled instead at the long grass and chewed the wheat-like heads, screaming inwardly at her, as she was screaming to me:

"I love you. I want to hold you. I want to feel you."

181

I had wanted to ask a thousand questions, but I could not bring myself to break this magic, singing silence in which we acknowledged to each other how loving we were. My voice had been lost in my bowels and any question I could have put would have broken the enchantment; we had been afraid to lose what little we had had, and rather than try for a better understanding, a clearer indication of our feelings, we had remained on the brink of our emotions. Had I spoken, I would have awakened reality and with it the attendant embarrassment of our situation. These first, deep stirrings of primitive emotion do not permit of words; words destroy instead of enlarging them. Words are for the sophisticated, the cultured, the degenerate refined; the primitive reaches out and touches and licks.

The twilight had deepened, lights had flickered on over the campus, it was becoming unwise to stay out alone together, side by side, in the dark. We had descended, stiff and chilled, into the valley where the college snuggled, and had muttered an indifferent good-night to each other at a halfway point in the quadrangle that divided our dormitories. Nothing had taken place, everything had happened. We had confessed to each other without speaking; we were now secure of each other and, at the same time, afraid.

The sequel to this had been a wretched episode and, as I recalled it, I wondered what intensification of it I should have to execute with you.

It concerned a bit of clay. Because of our very inarticulateness this girl and I had had to find some non-verbal, nondemonstrative way of expressing ourselves. I had taken refuge in romantic poetry which was duly published in the university magazine, and she in modelling; and she modelled, without my knowledge, a clay head of me, an uncannily good likeness invested with just that touch of understanding that distinguishes the able artist from the mere dilettante, and, naturally enough, this talent did not go unperceived. The whispers had begun among the faculty, for one art-teacher told another of the extraordinary work of her pupil, the head was recognized as mine, somebody remembered having seem us climb the hill behind the golf course at sunset and the scandal rolled around the campus gathering adherents like the snowball it was. Before anything had come to a showdown, the university semester had closed and she went to Florence during the summer to study. The following year she had remained in Paris, at the Sorbonne, as an exchange student, and only during the last year—our senior year—did I again see her. We had not communicated for the entire time of her absence and we now had pretended a mutual disinterest. My first glimpse of her, after the eighteen months' interval, had been a distant one; she had loped across the campus towards the chapel for the regular Sunday-evening organ recital.

I had followed her to the Bach concert and had sought her in the semi-darkness. She had slipped out before the conclusion of the recital and I had understood she was avoiding me. If she did not wish, or need, to see me how could I have confessed I wanted to see her? We had observed a system of evasion, although each constantly had looked for the other;

how could we have evaded had not each been everlastingly conscious of the other?

Just after the Christmas holidays, when the term had been almost half over, the yearly student art exhibition took place at which a prize was awarded for the best piece of creative art by a student of the university. I had been busy those days, for the campus life was providing me with a gay time and I had small interest in art exhibits—amateur displays, I had called them. When she had won the prize I was partly pleased, partly apprehensive; with what had she won the prize? I think I knew, before entering the exhibition gallery, what I would find.

My own head, in plaster, had looked back at me from under the prize-announcing plaque. It was an excellent likeness, by far the outstanding bit in the exhibition, and there could be no quibbling about the justness of the award. I had been pleased because of the double flattery: *she* had not forgotten *me* and *I* had had the good taste to select, from the swarms of students, an outstanding one. So much for my pleasure. I had been angry at the same time because I considered she had had no *right* to exhibit me without consulting me. I had been far too egotistical to recognize the plaster head as a love-offering, a tribute, a plea. I had seen in it nothing more than an unwarranted assertion of her superiority over me.

The scandal of sophomore year had been superseded by choicer gossip and the head had remained exclusively an art piece. It had been donated to the permanent university collection. We were both immortalized, as it were.

I had left this head alone on its pedestal until just before matriculation in the late spring. The evening before the senior students were to receive their diplomas, I had walked unmolested into the exhibition gallery of the university art library where, due to the excitement of graduation, I had found nobody, not even the janitor, and, marching up to the plaster head of myself, I had lifted it and thrown it to the ground, smashing it to fragments. As coolly as I had come, I left, switching off the lights and plunging the gallery into darkness.

The following afternoon the senior students had begun to stream away from the university, their diplomas packed in their trunks, their bills paid, their fond, proud parents waiting to herd them home. Apparently, nobody had yet discovered the broken head, the farewells and tears and exchange of addresses and promises to write were occupying everyone's attention. I had hoped to leave the campus without meeting her, although I secretly wanted an eleventh-hour encounter. I had been afraid my vandalism might be brought to light, and she might make a scene. Once I had left the campus behind, I did not care when the smashed head was found. A comment on the whole affair might then appear in the *Alumnae Magazine:* "Accident in Exhibition Gallery to Plaster Head." Nobody would give a second thought to such an item.

In the main building of the university there is a long and wide corridor with windows running on one side of it and with students' rooms and stairways giving off the other. The stairways are old-fashioned, encased behind swinging glass doors to avoid draughts, and turning at right-angles half-way between each floor. As the elevator had not been functioning that afternoon, I found I must walk up the five flights to my room. I had plunged through the swinging glass doors, shutting out the noise and chatter in the corridor behind me, and had bounded up the old, worn stairs, rounding the right-angle turn with the speed of a baseball player making first base. The stairwells were not lighted and, coming from the brilliant sun-flooded corridor below, my eyes had not been accustomed to the musty darkness. I had thought I was alone.

I had collided with her as neatly as a railroad train backs into its bumpers in a station: my body had been pressed against her, and had she not put an arm out to hold me I would have fallen down the stairs. I had clung with one hand to the banister, leaning backwards from her, looking up into her face; with the other hand I had clutched her shoulder for balance. After we had known each other for three years I was finally, and by accident, in the classical position of lovers, at the mercy of the one above me, encircled in a firm hold.

For the first time during the university year she had spoken to me.

"You broke the head," she had said, more as a fact than as an accusation. "Why?"

"You can't exhibit me as if I were a prize peony in a flower-show!" I had protested.

"But I did it to please you."

I had been prepared for the arguments, discussions, excuses, but not for so frank and revealing an explanation. Suddenly I had been very much aware of our proximity, of the slight wind-swept scent that emanated from her skin, of the texture of her silk blouse and the lines it covered without hiding, of her arm encircling me, of our legs pressed against each other's, of her soft, black hair curled upwards about her head like a sporty halo, of her white teeth so near to me that she had but to lean forward a trifle to bite me, of her eyes hard and clouded, of her breath brushing my face warmly and in that instant's awareness I had known that I faced the first emotional decision of my life. It is difficult to refuse a love that one has deliberately sought and I hesitated on the stairway for a few dangerous moments, feeling all the pent-up desires of three years welling up within me. Her arm no longer merely supported me, its pressure had become urgent; had anyone come along the stairway in those minutes we both might have had our diplomas revoked without so much as an explanation asked. We had been in a most compromising posture in a public place.

It is impossible to give any rational explanation of the why and wherefore of the intricate thought-process the mind enacts in those seconds when it is forced to a decision and has no time to reason. I only had known that this affair between us was ending, not beginning, with this embrace on the stairway and that I could go on to something better. Secretly, I had wanted this scene, this physical confession of desire; the uncorroborated knowledge had been insufficient. Secure now that in the past three years she had been in my blood as deeply as I in hers, I had felt capable of abandoning her;

it was not she herself I had wanted, it was the confession from her. The prize obtained, the game had been finished.

"You can't please me any more!" I had whispered up at her. "It's too late. It's over!" and I flung myself out of her arms to speed upstairs as if in flight. I had felt rather than seen (for I did not look back) that she remained motionless on the stairway. I had not meant to be cruel, I had been concerned only with what I had deemed best for me.

CHAPTER ELEVEN 🖋

I was ready to commit my crime (if indeed "crime" it can be called, for technically and legally I committed no crime whatsoever) long before the proper opportunities presented themselves for its execution. The success of this crime (I shall refer to it as a crime, for morally and socially it was one) depended, I was well aware, on my utilization of favorable circumstances. These circumstances, whatever they would prove to be, could not be forced; the delicate part of my criminal action was to wait for my chances, recognize and use them.

Despite forcing myself to be especially alert to everything that happened about me in the hope that a usable chance would swim within my reach, the days passed and nothing occurred. I was in a fever of impatience, for the danger you now represented to me grew daily and time was precious. I did not dare be with you for fear you might discover the power you had over me and I did not dare stay away from you for fear you would think my sudden unfriendliness strange. I contrived to see you mostly with other people before whom any private talk was impossible. The few times I came to your apartment I prepared myself beforehand, like a boxer entering the ring, to imagine everything you could do or say so that you would never catch me off guard. There comes a moment in loving when passion rides high and the world, public opinion and even life itself is well lost for the release from strain found in the coming together of two lovers. The world and public opinion I was quite prepared to lose, but not my life itself. I did not want to die for you or because of you.

During this time I thought of nothing and nobody except you. You were more than an obsession, you were a disease. You still obviously knew nothing about the novia and the stooge and you continued using her as a shield against me. You felt that so long as you could babble about marrying her you were safe from me. I came so near telling you the truth that I even had reduced the entire situation to a few pat words. "Listen, beloved, the novia wants to marry the stooge because she knows we love each other. Let's go away together to Timbuctu." How many times did I not start to tell you and then follow my "Listen, beloved" with something far less dangerous. "Listen, beloved, let's go to the opera." "Listen, beloved, let's have a look at the races." "Listen, beloved, let's go to the movies."

I was so close to giving in to you that I considered whether I had not better force the crime rather than wait interminably in the surety that at a certain point my resistance would snap and I should commit myself to the hell of living with you. Unexpectedly, and just when my desperation had reached its breaking point, my chance came, and not merely one chance but, after the long drought, there came a veritable rain of chances.

First, there was the business of the weather. That in itself should have been a sign to me, but I suppose, like everyone else, I took the weather for granted, something unalterable that signified little in my personal life. Autumn had come and the air was damp and chill; the whole city lay blanketed under a half fog and almost daily a light drizzle slimed down. In most big cities, London, Paris and New York, this cold wetness has its agreeable side; people wear furs, the houses are constructed to resist the penetration of the cold, there are fires in the hearths, the restaurants and stores are heated. In the temperate metropolis in which I lived the houses were built, oddly enough, as if the city were a tropical one, and although the high-ceilinged residences and public edifices resisted the summer heat they were ice-chests during the brief, clammy winter months, as cold and damp as the streets outside. During the late autumn and winter the entire city seemed to sniffle and cough and shiver; people

were pale, blue-nosed and rheumy-eyed, and the very buildings, never architecturally appealing, exuded an atmosphere
of grey and dismal desolation. Even the greatest optimist
would be subdued by this aspect of the quivering city, this
real misery, for the cold was never sufficiently severe to inflict genuine pain or hardship as is known in the snow-covered countries; the cold could not, in fact, even be termed
cold; it was the damp chill, the eternal wetness that depressed. The smells from the river and port drifted up
through the more fashionable parts of the city, the heavy
smoke of the factories did not rise but fell sootily over all
buildings impartially; a more melancholy scene would be
hard to visualize.

That this weather was the background for my crime never
occurred to me. In my home I was warm and comfortable; I
liked the dark, dreary days. Somehow, I could better stand
being separated from you in such weather, I was more mistress of my emotions. I desired you more, but needed you,
paradoxically enough, less. I sat before the fire in the music-
room and played endless sonatas and concertos on the gramophone, served tea to various intimates, discussed politics and
ethics and the latest books and newest fashions. I did what
civilized people have been perfecting for centuries, I led the
leisured life with grace and understanding, thanks to forty
years of appreciating it.

On Wednesday of a rainy week, I went to town to consult
with my old lawyer at the office. There was a matter of a
complicated contract to settle, one of those wranglings over
clauses that could not be arranged to the satisfaction of all

parties concerned. My old lawyer had made careful and detailed notes on the contract and had requested you to write up the final form and see to its signing. I had some money involved in the successful execution of the venture, but not very much, and it was money I was prepared to lose since it consisted entirely of dividends from bonds. For the company, the deal in question was of far more importance than it was to me.

I waited impatiently for the elevator in the marble hall of the business temple. Several times I pressed the button to summon the lift. One elevator was out of commission; there were only two, and the other was overworked with the demands of the business tenants. A telegraph messenger-boy came in and stood beside me, stamping his feet to keep warm and jabbing repeatedly at the bell. We entered the lift together and, as the doors closed, the telegraph-messenger asked the elevator-boy on what floor he could find you. He flourished a cable with your name on it for both the elevator-boy and me to read.

"Fourth?" he repeated after the elevator-boy, in a thick, adenoidal voice, and then settled himself in a corner.

"Where's it from?" the elevator-boy asked as the lift climbed slowly upwards.

"New York," the messenger-boy said carelessly. "It's a death notice."

"What kind of a notice?" I inserted quickly before the elevator-boy could speak.

"A death notice. *You* know," the messenger-boy told me,

193

winking across me at the elevator-boy. "It means a good tip," he added with practical satisfaction.

"How do you know it's a death notice?" I asked, my voice uncertain and a bit wavering.

"Lady, they tell me at the office," the messenger-boy explained patiently. "This gets delivered *in* person." He tapped the yellow cable importantly and made a slight bow to both the elevator-boy and me.

Stopping the elevator at the fourth floor, the elevator-boy paused before opening the doors. He made a tragic face, and, despite the insistent buzzing of waiting clients, seemed prepared to tell us a long story. He said he remembered when his mother had died, how hard it had hit him, and was all prepared to continue when the messenger-boy said:

"It's the father, not the mother."

That was even worse, the elevator-boy assured us as he slid the doors open; he could remember when his father died. While he was detailing his emotional reaction, I slipped out of the cage and walked down the hall to my old lawyer's office. Of course I found you with him, discussing the snags in the contract. I made a sign that you be dismissed, for I had no desire to have the messenger-boy trace you to this office where I would be obliged to watch you receive the bad news. As you gathered up your papers, I was struck by the extreme youthfulness of your movements. You looked, in that split second during which I observed you so concentratedly, elastic and almost boyish, and the knowledge that within a few minutes you would read the cable announcing your father's death made the difference between youth and age seem even larger. You were so flexibly alive, so clean and eager. And I felt again that surge of being old, being so much nearer to death than you and so much more accustomed to it. I think I sighed noticeably, for the old lawyer looked at me and asked me if anything were wrong.

I heard, as I looked over papers and legalities with the old lawyer, your hurried footsteps pass the door of the office and I knew you were leaving to go home. I dawdled over the business I had to attend until I thought you must have reached your flat and then I telephoned you, ringing steadily until you answered, your voice muffled and thick.

"I should like to see you right away," I said without preamble into the telephone.

"Not now, please. Any other time," you answered.

"I want to talk to you about your father," I amplified.

There was a long pause; you cleared your throat and then asked:

"How did you know?"

"Shall I come and see you now?" I answered your question with one of my own.

"Yes. Please," you replied and your voice sounded firmer.

When you opened the door of your apartment to my ring, I saw at once that you had been crying. I suggested you pour us both a drink, and while you fussed at the bar I glanced about the room. Every time I came to your apartment I had made it a habit to survey your room to notice any changes or improvements. Your desk, I saw, was in great disorder, the drawers opened and papers and photographs piled at random over its surface, almost sliding off. I sat beside you on the sofa, facing the desk, holding your hand in mine, and I asked you about your father. How had he died, had your mother sent the cable, what did you think her plans were, was there anyone else in your family who should be advised? While I asked and you answered, my eyes reverted continually to the untidy desk. I had no idea why the desk interested me so much, I was reacting purely as an animal; something on the desk demanded my attention. Even as I listened to you, encouraging you to talk, some other portion of my mind was at work, talking to me through your talk. My sympathies, my feelings were with you but my thoughts, despite myself, were elsewhere.

I was realizing, even as I held your hand, fondling it, that this day was the beginning of my active undertaking of my crime. The death of your father must somehow be utilized. Knowing how close you were to your father, I understood that his death would affect you deeply. The thing to do, my brain schemed, was to use this death as the first step on the road of reverses that would eventually push you into committing a drastic, desperate action. There must be no let-up in the series of calamities that should befall you. It must become my business to create calamities (had I not made rain? why then could I not do something simpler?). I must see to it that you sank into that kind of apathetic despair for which there is no remedy except to leave life behind. I must wind you in a maze of catastrophes until, confused, you would be driven to execute that idea which had always so attracted you and with which, in your darker moments, you coquetted: the idea of suicide. I must beat you to a pulp so that death would be a relief to you.

Looking at you next to me, talking haltingly and twining your fingers about mine as children do when they are in distress, I could feel the betraying tears rising hotly behind my eyes. I wanted to take you in my arms and comfort you and say, "But, beloved, you still have me, and we are young, and there is a long future ahead." But I wasn't so young and we had no possible future and, lastly, I was leaving you.

Looking back now over our relationship there seems to have been very little orthodox in it. We had made love in public and nobody had heard us; now, when I was taking leave of you, you were not even aware that I was going from you forever, never to return.

Sitting quietly next to you on the sofa, I gave you up, I allowed my intelligence (which could not be moved or swayed by your appeals, your physical presence, your voice, your smell and all the rest of it that reaches out and enslaves the sentiments) to take command. I had never lost sight of the fact that it was your life or mine, and even in this moment of loving you I yet loved myself more. The sense of self-preservation, in the last analysis, triumphs; it is only when we are thrown out of balance and do not think, as in war or flood or earthquake, that we forget this sense. In the calmness of your living-room there was no possibility of my forgetting it.

You continued to reminisce about your father. You described how he used to sit when he listened to music; suddenly you jumped up and said you would show me a picture of him he had just sent in one of his last letters to you. You rummaged along the over-crowded desk top, flipping papers about, and as you made further disorder in the chaos something dropped, slipping with a crackle, off the corner of the desk. It was a pink folder and its contents of papers spilled across the floor. I needed only a cursory glance to see it was the contract which you apparently had brought home with you. Impatiently you gathered up the thin sheets, crammed them on top of the folder and slammed them negligently on the desk. With your other hand you fished out the photograph and came across the room to show it to me.

I saw a tall, thin, stoop-shouldered edition of yourself, a credible replica of you at sixty-five. Although I concentrated on the snapshot and murmured the usual absurdities about similarity and handsomeness that one feels called upon to make in such circumstances, my mind was not on your father. I was scheming busily, for now I realized what I had been seeking in your apartment; it was the contract, and I had come, all unwittingly, to rob it from you, unaware, of course, that this was the real object of my visit. The contract with its imposing, flourishing signatures seemed to shrill at me from the desk. Its dim pinkness was so obvious to me that I thought you must *feel* the strident discord it was striking. *I had to steal it,* cleverly, suavely.

I have always affected large handbags and I noticed at once that I could stuff the papers, without the folder, into my bag with ease. I needed only the opportunity; somehow, I had to maneuver you out of the room, for the few seconds required for my successful confiscation.

". . . and Father particularly liked Bach. I suppose he educated me to Bach. Aside from Bach being the purest and noblest music there is," you were saying.

Like a stone, your reference to Bach fell into the black pool of my subconscious and caused waves of concentric ripples to flow towards the shores of my surface thoughts. Had I had any doubts as to the necessity of my stealing the contract, this reference to Bach dispelled them, for here I was back to the university again, the Sunday-evening organ recitals, the long years of hidden loving, the destruction of the plaster head. Here was the intensified parallel, the signpost screaming out at me: "Take it and save yourself. Take it and start things moving!"

I hesitated still within the protective, non-active circle of safety, postponing the unpleasant moment just a bit, and then, as if Fate itself had become impatient with me, the doorbell rang, three times in quick succession. I recognized the ring as your novia's; she had always rung the bell in my house like that, too.

You looked at me with wide eyes and asked, puzzled:
"But how can she know about it? Have you told her?"

I shook my head, my mind too busy to take time out for speech. Obviously, I thought rapidly, the novia knew nothing about your father's death. She had come to call on you for quite another reason, knowing you were at home, for your light was visible from the street below. The other reason could only be to tell you of her approaching marriage and to take her leave of you. If your novia came into the room I would never have an opportunity to be alone in it to steal the contract. I had to manage to be alone before she came. She repeated her triple ring, insistent, compelling. You jumped up from the sofa and started for the door, muttering,

"Well, I'd better let her in."

"Oh, darling," I cried out softly. "Don't let her see you like that, you look frightful. You better wash your eyes and smooth your hair." In desperation, I had hit upon the one appeal that I knew you would be unable to resist. Your vanity would triumph, even in the moments of this first sorrow. "I'll open the door," I offered, rising from the sofa, and as you turned towards me to go to the bedroom I held you an instant by the elbow and said, "Warm water takes away the marks of tears."

You smiled, said "Thanks" and closed the bedroom door. I heard your steps cross the uncarpeted floor to the bathroom. Jumping to the desk, I scooped up the contract and its attendant pink duplicates, folded the lot expertly and put them in my stiff, copious bag. Before the novia could ring again, I had skidded across the room and opened the door.

She was surprised and displeased to see me and hesitated in the doorway. It was I who invited her to come in, I who told her your father had died. I explained that I had dropped by to console you.

"Oh," the novia said in a girlish, breathy voice, "then I can't tell him!"

"What did you say?" I inquired tactfully, realizing perfectly she had called to confess her coming marriage to the stooge to you.

"I said, how did his father die?"

I accepted the substitution as if I truly had not heard what she had said and explained the details of the death to her. Even as I spoke you re-entered the room. She flew to you in a whirl of movement and was unashamedly in your arms before my eyes, gabbling how sorry she was, how she hadn't known, and was there anything she could do? As you disengaged yourself from her hold, I saw her face and I knew she was hoping for some excuse to stay with you, to find a reason to cancel her marriage vow, such as it was, with the stooge. She wanted you to need her, and in the moment when you might have needed her I was prudently (if by pure accident) on the scene, forestalling her. I was impatient at the expression on her face; it was obvious she had come to tell you something important and devastating, but you were so taken up with your father's death you did not understand the meaning of her look. You most assuredly missed the significance of her embrace and the lingering hands she rested on your arm.

"How did you happen to come?" you asked her.

"I . . . saw the light in your window from the street," the novia told you, fumbling for words, "and . . . just took a chance at finding you home. Wanted a . . . drink," she finished up and laughed unsteadily.

Oh, the drama of it, I thought disgustedly. What a wonderful third-act finale she had planned for herself in this flat, alone with you, and now, thwarted by me, she was obliged to keep silent. Her expression, her actions spoke eloquently, but you were not sensitive to anything save your father's death and you missed what she was telling you. This pawing over you, I thought furiously, watching her fingers fondle your sleeve, this physical last contact with you, this awful, dreary, passionate leave-taking, all naked and evident. Two leave-takings in one night, and you not even aware of it; I started to smile but checked myself as I remembered your father. But then, there is the old saw about how it never rains but it pours. Her hands dropped from your arm and she looked at you beseechingly; you noticed nothing, you were looking at the snapshot of your father lying on the cocktail-table.

"Isn't it strange," you said abruptly, "somebody dies and, suddenly, there's nothing left except some letters and photographs."

"There's always the influence," I inserted quickly.

You shrugged and stepped towards the table, leaving the novia stranded in the room behind you.

"The older one grows," you observed, "the more one is influenced by strangers and the less by one's parents."

How much longer, I thought to myself angrily, must I watch her agonize through her farewell? I had made no such fuss and certainly I loved you far more understandingly and intensely than the novia ever could. But then, I reflected, a bit sour-sweet, that was the difference between being forty, as I was, and being as young as the novia. At forty, one had learned to relinquish without benefit of flagellation, at twenty-five one still luxuriated in the masochism of mental and emotional torture. The novia, unwittingly, wrung her hands, that feminine gesture so peculiar to the very young

and very old women. If I could give him up quietly and
disciplinedly, I wanted to shout at her, so can you; stop this
romantic glubbering.

"Well," I said casually, "a visit is appropriate, but it becomes an intrusion at a time like this if protracted too long."
That will stop you, my girl, I thought craftily, and turned to
the novia. "Can I give you a lift to the station?" I asked her.
"I have a taxi waiting for me downstairs." This was untrue,
but I could always claim the cab had deserted me. The station was only a few blocks away.

The novia hesitated and then capitulated with a low,
"Yes, thanks, very kind of you."

We took leave of you together and, as she stepped aside
for me to precede her into the tiny elevator, she suddenly
threw her arms about you and kissed you, all tears and desire,
on your mouth. Wordlessly, I closed the elevator doors behind her as she swept into the lift. It descended slowly and
she sniffled and powdered her nose.

"Don't take it to heart so," I said kindly, putting a hand
on her arm. "After all, sixty-five isn't so young and his
father has had a good, full life. I know it's difficult not to
cry over a death, but it's useless, my dear. Death is one final-
ity that's not to be argued with."

The novia froze in the act of dropping her compact in her
purse. The lift had reached the ground floor but neither of
us made a move to open the grille doors.

"You know it isn't that!" the novia said, and for the first
time I heard her shrill voice descend to an ominous alto as
she fought to control herself. *"He* doesn't know, but you

know. I don't know how you know, but you do. You know everything."

I slid the elevator doors open and wanted to walk out but she detained me an instant, seemed on the point of speaking, and then followed me.

"The cab seems to have gone," I remarked, making a pretence of searching the street. "I suppose we might as well walk." I touched her arm and she obediently fell into step beside me. "We can cross diagonally through the park and save ourselves a beck," I said.

The night was damp and cold and we walked quickly and in silence. As we came to the park the novia stumbled and I steadied her. Passing under a street lamp I saw she was weeping. The gravelled path crunched under our high heels as we walked; damp and chill or not, the usual lovers huddled on the park benches, their unlicenced hands seeking the intimacy of each other's bodies. Suddenly the novia stopped and I, a few paces ahead, stopped too, turning to look at her, I thought she must have broken her high heels on the gravel. Instead, she stood very straight and defiant and her voice, again low, came to me, subdued.

"Have you ever wanted to kill anybody?" she asked me. "Murder someone, I mean?"

At her words my heart pounded maddeningly and I remember wondering if my furs would muffle the sound or if she could hear it. I paused deliberately before answering.

"No," I lied finally, as if I had considered the problem for the first time. "Have you?" I added interestedly.

"Yes!" the novia cried. "Yes, oh, yes!" and to my relief

she burst into sobs, miserable burning sobs that indicated very clearly her bewilderment and her frustration. "But I haven't the courage! I don't know how!" the novia went on; and then, in a strident voice that caused the indecent couples on the benches to pause in their sweet explorations, she cried, "Oh, I wish you would *die!*"

"*Me,* my dear?" I asked with gentle innocence. "Why *me?*"

"*You* know why, I *feel* you know why. I hate you and I'm all wrong to hate you, you've been so nice to me. But I hate you, you hear? I want to die!" and with this the novia sprang from me and ran towards the station. Had she run back to your apartment house I would have had to run after her, but as it was I let her go, following her flying figure as best I could. I saw her take a 'bus that went to the suburbs and I knew, as certainly as if she had told me, that she was going to the stooge. The marriage date would be determined right away.

I hadn't been home for more than half an hour when you telephoned me.

"I don't know what you'll think of me," your voice said over the wire, "but something terrible has happened. Maybe you can help me, if you've got a good memory."

"What's wrong?" I asked, knowing perfectly you had discovered the disappearance of the contract. "You know I have a good memory."

"It's about the contract," you said reluctantly. "You know which. Do you remember something fell off my desk this evening when I was looking for father's photograph?"

"Of course I remember," I assured you promptly. "It was some pink sheets in the folder."

"Right. What did I do with them?"

"You picked them up and put them on your desk," I told you.

"That's what *I* thought," your voice said. "I can find the folder but not the sheets."

"Look, beloved," I said into the receiver, "this is no time to worry about a contract. It must be there. Go to bed now and try to sleep and tomorrow you can worry about the contract. Do you know what I suggest? I suggest you drink eight whiskies. You'll have a headache tomorrow but you'll feel less pain elsewhere. I saw you put the contract on your desk so it must be there. Now drink and go to bed."

There was a silence at the other end of the line and you said, tired and relaxed: "What would I do without you?"

"I give my beloved sleep," I replied and hung up. I could feel my scalp prickling as the full import of my phrase struck me and I made a commotion out of dressing for a dinner party such as I had never before made. When the old lawyer came to escort me to the house of some important bore he found me peevish and snappy. Briefly, I wished the novia's desire might be realized; that night I felt like dying but I told myself all this was so much emotional weakness and it would be wiser for me to ignore my heart and bowels and concentrate on my plans. Over a stupid dinner I became the life of the party, but I was merely trying to drown out the word that galloped through my mind incessantly like a horse's hooves over harsh earth: sleep, sleep, sleep.

206

It's hard lines, of course," my old lawyer said to me (through long pulls at his malodorous cigar) a few days later when he came to call on me at the house to tell me about the loss of the contract, "and I don't like to crack down upon him at a time like this. I understand he was very fond of his father?" He looked at me inquiringly and I murmured that that was what I had been led to believe. "Remarkable," the old lawyer commented dryly. "Hardly would have believed it could still happen. However, he took the contract home with him, and now he can't find it. Ordinarily, I'd fire him for a mistake like that. It's costly and it's a nuisance. But, as I said, at a time like this . . ." he shook his head. "Well, my dear," in another tone of voice, briskly bantering as old men are apt to become with younger women, "after attending so many parties in succession I suppose tonight you'll catch up on your beauty sleep?"

"I hope to." I smiled back at him and wondered if the evening editions of the papers were yet out because then, in the "List of Travellers" which every newspaper affected I would be able to see if the novia and the stooge finally had left town to honeymoon in one of the four or five luxurious winter resorts of the country. Ordinarily I never troubled to read the columns of names in small type under *"Hotel Arrivals and Departures"* but tonight I planned to scan the list very carefully. I was impatient that my visitor leave. I yawned genteelly as a polite indication that I was truly and understandably tired, and after a few random comments the old lawyer left.

In my hurry to obtain the evening newspapers I rushed directly to the kitchen to ask the servants for them, but they had not yet been delivered. Angrily I resigned myself to waiting for them in the library.

You telephoned me before the papers were delivered. As soon as I heard your voice I knew that my foresight had been correct indeed. You were almost incoherent with anger, dismay, chagrin and a stubborn refusal to believe.

"Have you seen the evening papers yet?" you asked me

without troubling to observe any of the amenities of greeting.

"No. Is there something special I should look for?"

"Something special?" you echoed, and your voice almost broke in fury. "Look under *'Hotel Arrivals and Departures.'* They've gone away together, they're honeymooning on a ski-trip!"

"Are you drunk?" I asked sharply into the telephone, thinking that to be the most logical and innocent (and convincing) query I could make.

"Drunk!" you repeated. "I'm drunk with rage if you call that drunk! My best friend! I didn't think they even liked each other!"

"What are you talking about?" I asked patiently, and you told me, in fits and starts and expostulations, that you had just read of the civil wedding of the stooge and your novia in the local paper and that under the *"Hotel Arrivals and Departures"* they were listed as guests who had flown down to stay at one of the most expensive and luxurious winter resort hotels in the south.

"Of course it would be a ski-trip," you said bitterly. "After all, he's a champion skier, and why shouldn't he want to show off before the new bride even if she's never been on skis in her life!"

"It's somewhat unexpected news," I said after a little pause, "but why are you taking it so hard? If you love her you should be glad she's married your best friend. And if friendship is all you claim it is you should be glad he's got her! What better could you wish for him?"

"But the secrecy!" you protested. "Behind my back! Why didn't they tell me?"

"They surely had their reasons," I defended the couple.

"And so young," you went on, paying no attention to me; "mere children. How can they be married? They're five years younger than I, both of them."

"And four years over the age of consent," I pointed out, wanting to laugh.

"But why didn't they tell me? Why?"

"I don't know," I said. "Now, look here, my dear, I know this has upset you, but there is something else disagreeable in the air. Have you found the contract?"

"The contract?" I could tell by your voice your thoughts were far from the contract. "No," you confessed sullenly. "I've found only the folder." When I made no reply to this you called suddenly into the telephone, "Listen! Can I come and see you? Now, right away?"

"You're much too upset," I evaded. "You'll say all kinds of things for which you'll be sorry. Furthermore, I'm in bed. If you like we'll talk it all over tomorrow."

"I'm going after them!" you exploded into the telephone. "That's what I'm going to do!"

"Suppose we lunch together tomorrow?" I suggested in a polite, matter-of-fact voice.

"You mean talk in public? You don't want to come to the apartment?" You sounded incredulous and wheedling at the same time.

Certainly I wanted to come to the apartment for the pleasure and excitement of being alone with you, but that was far too dangerous for me. A public lunch in my most elegant costume with a brimmed hat to hide my face if need be and in one of the modern mirror-lined restaurants in town (so that I could watch myself and be sure to play my part well) was far more advisable.

"I'd love to come to your apartment but I haven't time. I'm in town all day tomorrow so lunch is about all I can manage."

"In town tomorrow?" you objected. "It isn't Wednesday."

"When unexpected things happen," I said smoothly to you, "like the loss of a contract, I'm obliged to change my program a bit, you know."

That sobered you; it was a wicked thrust. I had nothing to do in town the following day and I had no intention of bothering with the contract. I had fabricated a cloth of lies for you and you were forced to accept them.

"Lunch it is," you agreed. "Anywhere you say," and I could tell by the controlled evenness of your voice how deeply hurt you were.

I arrived before you at the fashionable restaurant I had deliberately selected and, consulting with the head waiter, I chose a table facing a mirrored column in which I could observe my own reflection. I ordered lunch for both of us, picking dishes I knew you liked, and then I sat in the bar, in one of the overstuffed easy chairs, waiting for you, combed and groomed and gowned to perfection the better to contrast with you, for I knew you would arrive flushed and a bit rumpled from the office and would feel just slightly inferior escorting someone as impeccably turned out as I.

You had your complexes and now I did not hesitate to capitalize on my knowledge of them. Clothes, it has been said repeatedly, make a man; they do more than that, they create a mood, set a tempo, and they can undermine confidence as well as impart it. Today, I resolved, you were to be very conscious of the difference between us, of my savoir-faire, my clothes, my wealth, all in brilliant contrast to your worriedness and your salary.

You were late and came rushing into the restaurant with that lovable and ridiculous impatience of excited youth. You hesitated a fraction of a second on seeing me and then wordlessly thrust a battered newspaper at me. Of all the men in that stylish, high-priced restaurant I think you were the only one to carry a newspaper; the playboys who toyed with rare foods in such a modish atmosphere were above the mundane reportage of a daily; they read about themselves in the glossy monthly society magazines.

"Let's have drinks at our table," I said to you. "I haven't much time so I've taken the liberty of ordering a table and lunch along with it." I preceded you into the glittering mirrored dining-room, leaving the smoke and chatter of the equally glittering bar behind. In the mirrors I saw you following me, looking at me with a curious and puzzled penetration.

"You're so fancy," you observed as we unfolded our stiff white napkins after ordering cocktails. "I suppose this really is your setting," and you nodded at the pretty tables with their bowls of hot-house roses and the decorative women smiling and nodding at their paunchy escorts, "but somehow I never associate it with you." You sighed and then appraised me, rather more coolly than I had expected. "You look lovely and distant," you said finally. "I never realized how well diamonds suit you."

"It's never too late to notice," I remarked, and unfolded the newspaper you had brought me to read an item you had marked in red. It was the newspaper for which your novia had worked and they had given her a generous write-up along the lines of "cub reporter snatches millionaire's son." There was a photograph of her; she looked smilingly young and happy. After I had read the article I refolded the paper and handed it back to you.

A pale-green frosted drink, as exotic as the restaurant itself, was set before me and I regarded it thoughtfully, waiting for you to speak. You had asked to see me; it was up to you to make the first move.

"Look at me, please!" you ordered suddenly, curtly, and I raised my head in surprise.

Your eyes were very wide and green, something like the translucent color of the cocktail, and, like the drink, wet, for the tears lay without overflowing. The elaborate setting receded and I found I was, as I had tried to avoid being, alone with you, removed from the surroundings, blind to the mirrors and the diamonds and hot-house roses. I was being pulled towards you.

"Do you know what I thought last night after I spoke to you?" you asked.

"No, how can I know?"

"I was thinking that something, somewhere, is completely

wrong in my life and I don't know how to fix it up. I feel as if everything I do will end badly. You can't just ignore feelings like that, can you?" you asked me almost belligerently. "If I don't lose my job because of having mislaid that contract I shall lose it because of some other stupid, inexplicable mistake. And then, everything seems to be happening to me at once. My father held the family together, you know, and now that he's dead the family will fade away—what's left of it. I don't have a wife to turn to, not even a loyal friend." You grimaced wryly as you said *loyal friend*. "And you," you added, but without even a hint of reproach in your voice, simply as if you were stating an uncontradictable, well-established fact, "abandoned me long ago."

"You are imagining things," I told you shakily.

"This morning," you went on, "I woke up after dreaming that my Ming vase had broken and I rushed to the living-room to see if it was still there. If my good-luck piece breaks, it's the end."

"Was it there?"

"Yes."

"You see," I said with more confidence, "you are over-wrought. I know it's been hard for you, your father's death, and this business about the contract, and now the marriage, but I'm sure your bad-luck streak is at an end."

"It isn't a question of luck," you contradicted me. "I feel that somebody or something is working against me. Can you understand that, or is that too much for your practical mind?"

"It doesn't sound very logical," I replied, and wondered

if the color had flooded my face because I had become hot with fear and excitement and I could feel my satin blouse sticking to my damp skin.

I examined you avidly, anxious to discover if you suspected me of having a hand in your bad-luck streak, and you looked calmly back at me.

Why was it that I could never gaze at you impersonally, finding your features powerless to interest me any longer? In almost all love-affairs there comes that point when the passionate attention of the lovers declines and they find, against their will and to their horror, that each bores the other, that there is no longer anything to say, that the excitement has evaporated and that it is impossible to recapture those sweet and stimulating palpitations which had made living such a thrilling experience. Looking at you, I was each time forced to succumb again to the charm of your glance and the irresistible (however absurd) fascination of your person. In a way I was constantly relieved to discover I still loved you as intensely and unreasonably as ever—it spoke well for my zest for living; on the other hand, I was repeatedly chagrined at my inability to escape you.

Were you worth me? More accurately, had you the right so much as to know anyone like me? Did you deserve my love and interest? With each little crisis it became increasingly evident you did not. I am a fighter, not in the physical field of jaw-busting and belly-punching but in that subtler ground where the inner personality strikes out to assert itself. The physical maneuvers of armies on a battlefield are still so much primitive mathematical shifting of strategies the better to attack when compared with the complex and almost fluid shiftings and reformations and regrouping we exercise daily. The inner personality is at once general, artillery, cavalry and foot. His only difficulty is to follow the orders he himself gives for the successful realization of his own campaign. You were no fighter; your antennae warned you of calamity and instead of planning to avoid or defeat it you began to educate yourself to accept it. I am forever endeavoring to escape and to master my destiny, you were constantly preparing yourself to become resigned to yours. I am active, you were passive. I am trying to use the world, you permitted the world to use you.

However my mind might depreciate you, my senses, devoid of reason, admired you increasingly.

You began to break a wooden match into three equal parts, lowering your head to concentrate on this diversion.

"Have you ever thought," you asked me finally, as you arranged the splinters parallel to each other, "about the significance of white?"

"White?" I echoed, at a complete loss.

"White is for winding sheets, for example," you said cheerfully, "and one sends white flowers to funerals."

"To weddings, too," I pointed out, protesting and sarcastic.

"The death of the bachelor, the death of the virgin," you retorted imperturbably with a quick side glance at me.

I wondered what you were leading up to; that death preoccupied you was, by now, something I assumed as a matter of course. But what had white to do with it?

"It's clean, that's a great advantage," you observed, reflectively, "and if one is going to die," you continued slowly and with a certain degree of caution in your voice, "at a time designated by oneself, one ought to pick a clean and pleasant way."

"Who's going to die at a time designated by himself?" I asked irritably and yet with secret excitement because your procrastinating fumbling around this point was a torment to me.

"Why shouldn't *I?*" you asked. You emphasize the *I;* in the moral *should* you had no interest.

"No reason," I told you steadily, "if you feel you want to."

"You'd hardly miss me, would you?" you blustered at me, your annoyance evident in your voice.

"I've never tried to keep you from doing something you have wanted to do," I reminded you.

You looked at me with anger blazing in your eyes; you had expected me to argue, and now you felt I wasn't taking you seriously enough. I was deliberately goading you, I wanted to push you to a threat of suicide that you yourself would feel had to be made good. You reached for another matchstick and again broke it in three. When you spoke again, the anger had evaporated and your voice was even and controlled.

"I shall take the snow," you said. "It's the cleanest."

For an instant I was so startled that I did not think of snow but of the slang term for cocaine, and I believed you were considering drugging yourself to death. Then I saw the logic of your deductions and I began, foolishly, to twist my hands in my lap under cover of the white shroud of tablecloth. The novia and stooge were skiing and you had said, the previous evening, you would follow them. Was it possible, I thought uneasily, that the novia and not I was driving you to death, that you were willing to die on her honeymoon in order to embarrass and poison her the rest of her life? This was winter, of course, and there was no doubt about the easy possibility of becoming lost in the mountains and freezing to death during a long black night while the skiers, miles away, cocktailed and dined and danced in the fashionable hotel. Snow was clean and painless, that was incontestable.

It had been a long time since I had had anything to do with snow; in the temperate climate of the city snow never fell and in winter it was necessary to travel for hours before reaching a place where it was possible to walk in the snow. The nearest I had come to snow during the last few years had been as a spectator admiring a snow-tipped volcano or a white-capped mountain range. I had not touched snow for over a decade.

As a child, living in a cold northern country, I had adored the snow, as I think most children do, and had regarded it as something delightful. Even during the university years, snow remained a kind of gigantic and innocent plaything, and in my travels to winter resorts it had figured primarily as a convenience for amusing myself at certain sports. I can honestly say that that day, in the heated restaurant, lunching with you, was the first time I seriously considered snow as a killer instead of a playmate. I believe I was, for some minutes, more shocked by this new aspect of my old friend, the snow, than I was by your often-repeated hint of suicide.

"But what are you thinking of?" I blurted, sounding unconvincing, breathless and theatrical even to my own biased ears.

"What would you have me do?" you shot out at me impatiently. "Have me die under your nose by inches? If I had some dreadful and incurable physical disease, a cancer or a leprosy, let us imagine, you would hardly be so squeamish. Has it ever occurred to you that such physical things have their mental counterpart? It's possible to have a cancer of the mind, a leprosy of the will."

"But you were all right last week!" I shouted in stupid protest.

"What do you know about it?" you returned rudely, piling the six match splinters into a little heap. "I'm sorry," you said stiffly. "There are certain subjects that conventions tabu. Death by volition is apparently one of them. Old women can discuss their operations over teacakes but young men may not mention their fatal illness at luncheon."

"What are you talking about?" I demanded angrily. "What fatal illness? What melodrama is this?"

You tapped your forehead, then tapped your heart and leaned towards me.

"All deaths are melodramatic. Except the deaths of children, death is always an anticlimax. The line has snapped between head and heart," you told me; "there is no more will and I am too tired to desire. I am defeated, I retreat. The enemy has the field."

"What enemy?"

You frowned and said slowly:

"That's the one thing I don't know. I've never seen the enemy. It's been present a long time. What have I done, or what have I failed to do to bring this on myself?" You fiddled with the matches. "Perhaps the enemy is myself, or part of myself?" you suggested. "Oh, for God's sake!" you cried out, suddenly impatient. "Stop looking so startled and offended! What's strange in talking about death? It's as common as birth and you'd make no fuss over *that,* would you?"

The strangeness in talking about death lay in the setting, for the restaurant made our talk seem like a dialogue from some sophisticated play in which neither the audience nor the actors took the lines seriously since both knew there would be another performance the following evening at eight-forty. So long as one is not obliged to see or hear or smell death, death remains unreal. One cannot imagine the world continuing after one has died. To the healthy, life is so precious and wonderful that the very idea of anybody wishing to die is beyond their understanding; death has reality only for the suffering and the poor, and since few of us in the Western world are perpetually suffering nor everlastingly poor, death is real only some of the time. In disasters, where death is wholesale and gargantuan, it numbs us so completely that we react like automatons, firmly believing everyone can die about us but we are inviolable, immortal. When we survive and survey our bereavedness, then death has become real. But here, in a restaurant, well-fed, opulent in luxury, death was rather a dangerous and faintly naughty subject, like birth-control or the discussion of the thirty-six sexual positions.

"Since one has to die," you went on in an altered voice, quietly and almost conversationally, "it seems to me more sensible to die when one *wants* to rather than wait for some inauspicious moment when one might resent dying."

"But people want to die for better reasons than you have!" I argued.

"You say that because you don't recognize my reasons; they aren't parading before you in the usual form, but they are the real reasons that make people want to die, whatever other seeming ones are pushed forward to make the whole thing plausible. And forgivable."

"What are the real reasons?"

"Pain, tiredness, disgust. Most of us don't die of big, important things. We are worried or hounded to death by the trivial, our life has been gnawed away, we are eroded into nothingness," you answered. "Played out, I believe you would say," you concluded.

"At your age!" I mocked.

You looked at me with amusement and then said:

"Isn't there some saying about a man being as old as he feels?"

"But you have no right to die!" I protested.

"You mean, I have no right to live," you corrected.

"But think of all the people who have died who haven't wanted to die, soldiers in wars and travellers in accidents, people who have had death forced on them."

"It isn't the dying they objected to, I imagine," you observed, "it's the way they had to die. Nobody wants to die in the storm and discomfort of battle, nor in the unpreparedness of accidents either, for that matter. But since dying is inescapable, better we arrange for our deaths as carefully as we arrange for our living. And do you think," you asked me earnestly, leaning a bit towards me, "do you think that in *my* living I can in any way make up for their deaths? That's what their wives do, and all the beloveds left to sorrow and immortalize, the family, the friends, the sweethearts, living their lives in such a way so that the departed won't have died in vain. Plain, ordinary guilt feeling. It's they, you see, who invented the hero's death; the man who dies is to himself no hero. He's an unlucky devil getting it in the neck. But since there are wars and accidents, death has got to be made reasonable and so we have the phrases about "for God and country" or "died while scientifically experimenting" or "killed in opening new world travel routes," and so on, and that helps foster the idea that even in death one gets something in repayment. Actually, dying is the one act we commit for which we are not paid. And, ironically, death doesn't affect us, it affects those who cared for us. We die and that's the end, but for those who knew us and didn't die, there's the misery. They remember us and make themselves unhappy. That's why I say there's no payment for dying, for surely, if there were, in dying we would ask that those who love us don't mourn us, don't grieve. Of what use to us is their grieving?"

"Are you afraid of being mourned, or is it you are afraid there is nobody to mourn you?" I asked.

222

"You forget my ego dies with me," you answered, "so that problem won't arise."

"It seems so wrong to die," I remarked helplessly.

"On the contrary. It seems wrong to live as I do. And since I can't change that, better to die than to live wrong."

I shook my head at you.

"I'll live any way I can, right or wrong; I'm concerned with living, on any terms, at any price," I told you.

"What do you still want, then?" you asked, almost lazily. "Only the grabbers want to double what they have when they have everything."

To that I had no ready answer. There was, indeed, in my life nothing missing, possibly because I had learned to limit my horizons to the obtainable, possibly because Fortune had, as legend says she can, smiled on me.

But "having everything" by no means jaded me. I enjoyed the "having." The unending succession of sun and stars and wine and food, day and night and music and digestion, activity in the bright air and dreaming sleep, all these, instead of consuming my vitality with their sameness—as they consumed yours—augmented it, and I could find no words grand and powerful enough to convey to you my joy in the sun and the warmth, and in myself as a living being.

That anything with limits is a prison I did not deny, and certainly the world is geographically a limited place exactly as man himself is a limited being. I had accepted these limits as pleasant and unalterable, both those of the world and my own, whereas you, apparently, had found the limits strangling, stiflingly unbearable. In the end, perhaps the difference between us consisted in that we were two expressions of the same personality, yours a dark and somber manifestation of it and mine bright and lively. No doubt a successful fusion of our two interpretations of ourselves would have produced a balanced, integrated personality. Fortunately the perfect man or woman does not exist and we can continue, probably forever, the fascinating study of our imperfections which, in the final analysis, are what cause differences in the behavior of human beings. Perfection would always react the same; imperfection is divertingly and sometimes dangerously unpredictable. So long as we are man and not God our variations, slight and miserable as they may be, exclude the possibility of repetitions. Probably one needs a special disposition, a willing scrutiny to observe the variations; if so, you lacked that disposition.

"But think of all you'll be missing. There's so much ahead," I began persuasively.

"There's nothing ahead except repetition of what's already behind. You don't expect me to eat the same dinner twice over, do you, so why do you expect me to live the same life twice over?"

"I thought I had convinced you there was no such thing as exact repetition," I reminded you.

"There was a chance to avoid it, but you cancelled that chance. Without it, or, rather, not having been able to take it, I sink back into the old groove; dull business in a tenth-rate firm, breakfast-lunch-and-dinner, saying stupidities to thin women so they'll sleep with me, playing the second thousandth game of tennis, tying my shoelaces for the nine thousandth time in the morning."

"Bored to death," I inserted and stopped short.

"Boredom is a disease; most people are bored and hurry off to the movies or the nearest bar or the racetrack to escape boredom. Boredom means one cannot be alone with oneself. I've become so uninteresting to myself that I can't live with myself any more and the movies and the horses and the whiskies no longer attract. How stupid you are!" you observed impersonally. "Forever examining life and never considering death."

I smiled at you, for, ever since knowing you, I had considered death detailedly, your death to be sure, not my own, and you had not stumbled upon my designs.

"So there is nothing you are sorry to miss?" I pressed you. You shook your head.

"Possibly the concerts at the opera-house this winter," you replied, half-laughing. You hesitated a minute, seeming to reflect, and then said, "Have you ever noticed in the opera-house that ring of composers' names up in the ceiling with Verdi in the middle? Did you notice they left out Bach entirely? Imagine it! Meyerbeer in thirty-inch-high letters and no Bach. Have you ever noticed?" You stared at me unblinkingly, and I began to suspect you knew all about my use of the circle in the opera-house ceiling. "Of course you've noticed," you answered for me, "of course!"

"No, I can't say I have," I mumbled. "But I'll look next time."

You began to laugh delightedly, throwing back your head

and looking down your nose at me. You knew I had lied, and I knew you knew.

"Well," you said, "shall we go, or shall we discuss death some more? Would you like another coffee?"

"No, thank you." I consulted my tiny wristwatch, refraining with an effort from squinting. Whatever time it was, the moment finally had come when I must say "I go; good-bye," or the same couched in lengthier terms, and that would mean that our story was over, all except for the climax at which I would not be present and with which I could have nothing to do. How hard it is to leave the beloved. I avoided looking at you, pulling on my gloves carefully. "I must run along," I told you in a gossipy tone, and fussed with my bag, with the veil of my hat.

We walked out of the restaurant together. I signalled the doorman to get me a taxi, declining a lift in your car. You helped me into the cab and still I could not look at you. I thought you must speak to me, if only to produce the conventional parting, but you stepped back from the cab door in silence and my driver, racing his motor, slid away from the curb. I did not look back at you. We had parted, such parting as it was, in silence.

I had myself driven to your apartment and rang your doorbell confidently. The dusky maid unlatched the door cautiously, and, recognising me on the landing, opened it wide and stepped back, telling me a bit shyly you were not at home. I simulated surprise, hesitated, and then said you probably had been detained and I would wait for you in your living-room. The little maid asked if she could bring me something, a cup of coffee perhaps, and I declined quickly. I heard her working beyond the kitchen and concluded she was doing your washing.

I studied the Ming vase a long time before approaching. It glimmered among the dark books, aloof and cool in its private compartment, conspicuous in its beauty; it was a lovely, lovely thing.

The apartment about me seemed hollow and expectant. I was tempted to rehearse and dramatize all that had happened between us within these walls but dismissed such a sentimental luxury as being too cheap for me. The thought crossed my mind that possibly I had no right to kill you, herding you to your own death, but this, too, I dismissed, telling myself that my life was more important to me than yours was and I had every right, even every obligation, to preserve it.

I took the vase in my gloved hands and then crossed to your bathroom to wrap it in a towel. It seemed somehow improper to break it in the bathroom, a lack of finesse, and I went to your bedroom, surveying the room rapidly for a good place to break it; I settled upon the corner of your bureau. I swung the towel, with the vase wrapped in it, against the wood, hearing the dull thud as the vase broke, seeing the towel lose its form. I spread the towel on your bureau top, opening it cautiously; I felt the broken pieces of the vase in my hands and experienced a moment of panic. *This* was my murder, this disintegration that I had wreaked. For an instant I held the fragments of the crumpled vase in my hands and then began to sort the pieces from the crumbs of powder. Taking only the pieces I returned to the living-room and arranged them around the black lacquered foot on which the vase had stood. The porcelain crumbs I washed down your drain and I rehung your towel in the bathroom as I had found it. I sat on your chair by the desk for a few minutes, disconcerted to find that I was breathing too fast and that my knees were weak and my hands trembling. I counted the articles on your desk in an attempt to bring myself to normal. The little maid began to sing in the kitchen, rather sweetly, in a tremulous, girlish voice.

Feeling more confident, I rose and went to seek her out. She was ironing a shirt of yours and looked almost frightened at my intrusion. I opened my purse composedly and extracted a very large bill from my wallet and laid it on your shirt, even feeling the warm material through the fingertips of my glove. I watched her eyes widen with surprise and her lips part almost sensually.

"One could do a lot with all that money," I observed, and I met her look calmly. She realized, I saw, that this was a bribe and anxiety struggled with desire over her features. "Don't you have a sick mother?" I asked. "One of my maids once did."

"My brother," the little maid whispered.

Mother or brother, what was it to me except a corroboration that she needed money. I explained to her that by accident I had broken the white vase in your living-room and I preferred she took the blame for it.

"The white vase on the bookcase?" she cried. "But he warned me about it!"

"That's why it's a big note instead of a little one," I told her, and nodded to the green bill lying limply on your shirt. I noticed irrelevantly it lay beside your embroidered initials.

"Yes," the little maid said with a long sigh that the poor with consciences give as a sign of reluctance when they succumb to the bribe.

"I doubt he'll be as angry as you think," I told her and turned into the hallway and let myself out of your apartment. The little maid depressed me, accustomed as I was to the ceremony of bribes. Perhaps, I thought, as I walked down the steps of the building, this was her first bribe. I felt sorrier for her than for you until I realized I was using her to keep myself from thinking of you.

CHAPTER THIRTEEN

*R*eaching home,
I found to my surprise that my evening clothes had been prepared for me and one of the maids reminded me I was due to dine at a neighbor's, an engagement that had slipped my mind entirely. I welcomed this unexpected diversion, it would prove a help to me in avoiding any active thinking about you. I carried the idea of you in the back of my mind at all times, but this was in no way disturbing; you upset me only when you intruded to the fore.

No doubt in reaction to the afternoon and in a desperate attempt to keep you from pushing yourself forward in my thoughts, I set a gay tone for what ordinarily would have been a fairly conservative dinner party, and my hosts and their guests followed my lead enthusiastically. Although I did not stint myself on the wines and brandies I was careful not to drink too much for fear your name might slip from me; I was like a private detective standing guard over myself.

When the talk turned to the sailing boats that several of the men owned I claimed, in one of those rash and boastful moments we each fall into at times, that I was an excellent sailor and one of the guests bet me a large sum I couldn't man a catboat he had in the suburban harbor and take her out onto the river. I doubled the bet and said I would give the proof right then and there; who would come with me to the river?

There were some sensible but half-hearted attempts to torpedo this wildness but on the whole everyone was as anxious for excitement and diversion as I was. It is odd how the exaggerated mood of one person can infect an entire gathering until the prevailing group-mood becomes as exaggerated as the instigating mood. In evening-dress we entered the cars parked before the house and drove the few blocks downhill to the river and the little village cove where the white boats lay idle in the still wintry night. I wore a white dress which someone remarked would make my movements easy to follow, but, with the full moonlight, visibility in any case was good.

There was much shouting, and the corner policeman, on sleepy night duty, came to the wharf to investigate and then stayed to watch. I was rowed in a dinghy to one of the cat-boats, a clean-painted little ship that smelled spicy in the cold air. As if to assist me, a tiny, favoring wind ruffled the diminutive harbor. I began, in the moonlight, to fumble with the ropes and the stiff sails. The outlet to the river was not more than fifty feet from where the boat was anchored and I could steer an unobstructed course to it. The dinghy and its owner bobbed gently up and down on the long slow waves a few yards from me. Here was one sport, I thought, as I loosened the canvas, hauled in the anchor and prepared to do the work of two in manning the small boat, here was one sport we had never done together, you and I; we had never sailed, and this senseless night sailing of mine before an inebriated audience was simply to prove to myself that I was independent of you.

I shoved the tiller to my left and the boat glided slowly and at an imperceptibly slight angle to the outlet. I looked quietly back at the dinghy and, as I passed through the wet stone walls that guarded the entrance to the protected cove, I had the feeling that I was escaping, escaping all the bond-ages that tied me to the earth. Every sailor, alone in com-mand of his boat, knows that illusion, for the escape is al-ways temporary; inevitably, barring shipwreck, one returns to the land.

There was more wind on the river but nothing that could drive the boat quickly, and as we moved, the boat and I, I noticed that the catrig hardly swayed, and the canvas seemed painted against the night. There was something trance-like in this trip.

From the shore various voices in the group began to shout at me and I saw disembodied arms wave and gesticulate; the cajoling voices carried clearly to me; they called to me to turn and come back. I wanted to ignore them and sail on but I knew I could easily be overtaken in one of the motor-boats of the harbor. I relinquished my fantastic, dreamy position and set to work turning the little boat, scrambling about speedily in my efforts to be in two places at once. Against the slight wind, I began to tack, and, as I headed outward, I heard one of the women shriek at me to come in, and then a man's voice, indistinct, began to explain to her I was not running away but setting a zig-zag course to the inlet. How did the fool think one sailed against the wind, I thought irritably. The little boat leaned to one side behaving at last more like a true sailing ship than like a toy. I heard the water shiver past me, sibilant and eerie; it would take me over twice as long to return as it had taken me to go out. They would freeze on the wharf; let them freeze in their furs. Then I was conscious that I was not cold although I wore no wrap and my dress was of a thin material. The blood seemed to sing in my veins; the river, the boat, myself, the slowly swinging boom, the canvas, even the racks on the floor, we were all one, interdependent on each other. I swung the tiller to my right and the little boat, like some obedient domestic animal, headed for the stone-walled cove entrance glistening in the moonlight. As I slipped through we diminished what slight speed we had, shut out from the

233

help of the breeze, and I floated into the bay towards the anchoring buoy in a kind of intensified slow-motion. I hoped I had lost you forever on the river, shaken off the ghost of you, as it were. I felt that having dared the river and the night and the solitude I had engineered a great change and that of course everyone would immediately notice, when I stepped from the boat, that I was a different person, that I had drowned some heavy sorrow and returned to land with renewed vigor, that I was younger, gayer, freer, that having buried you in the water I was again myself.

There was applause from the wharf above me and, as I was rowed to shore after helping the owner take in his sails and fasten them, the group burst into song, the policeman singing with them. Over in the east, beyond the edge of the wide, placid river, the sky was lighting with the first grey of the winter dawn.

They welcomed me back boisterously, and I was shocked that they saw no change in me, that they were under the impression I returned to them as the same woman who had set out on the river. I could not understand their stupidity and blindness and I was brusque and at the same time enormously exhilarated. I had not expected *them* to change while *I* changed on the river, but I had expected them to notice the difference in me. As they treated me exactly as they had before my escapade, I began to feel myself sucked back into the old sameness, the river receded and the group reclaimed me as their own.

We went to a small bistro for hot coffee and bread and scrambled eggs. I felt giddy and wild, partly at having won so large a wager, partly at being the center of attention, the instigating force of the gathering, partly from the physical exhilaration of the sail and still because I had not resigned myself to returning to the group. There had been no craftsmanship to my performance, the night was so calm any child could have taken the catboat into the river and brought it back, but the fact of my having done so in evening-dress and from moonlight to dawn lent a certain unjustified glamour to the episode. I was in no mood to break up the party; I wanted to continue on this unreal plane of excitement.

In the harsh early light the women looked drawn and tired whereas I felt that I looked fresh and eager. I could feel vitality, like liquor fumes, pour out of me and I was well aware that the men looked at me admiringly and warmly. You see, I was shouting inwardly at you, you see how easily replaceable you are! I don't even miss you! I've crossed you out of my life already, already!

One of the guests, a grass-widower, drove me to my home, a man I had known casually for years whose mouselike wife gave periodic teas to which I was invited and which I seldom attended. The man himself had come occasionally to the house to play tennis but I had never played alone with him. Now he suggested, as he helped me from the car, that we have a game of singles on my tennis court and in my exuberant mood I was delighted with the prospect. Tennis was one of your sports, but this morning I could do anything you had ever done, and do it as capably as you. And, indeed, I played admirably and tirelessly on the court, arousing genuine compliments from my opponent. Later we drank beer together in the sun. I talked recklessly, wishing to hold this man with me; I feared to be alone.

When my guest, in his borrowed tennis clothes (he had played, I noticed with amusement, in a pair of your old shoes which you must have left behind you in the dressing-room), had left me, my exhilaration petered out. I was tired when I went to the telephone to ring the office and find out if you were there. When I heard, as I expected, that you were not, I tried your apartment, and there the familiar voice of the young maid told me you had taken the plane the preceding afternoon for the south. You must have left, I thought wearily, only a few hours after I quitted your flat. And you were by now on your skis, climbing through the snow. I trailed to my bedroom and flung myself, in my tennis clothes, across the bed and fell at once into a deep, uneasy sleep, the product of combined physical exhaustion and too much drink.

It was dark when I awoke, and I found myself covered by a fur rug which one of the servants no doubt had thought to throw over me. There was an almost terrifying heaviness to my body, as if all my limbs had become paralyzed, and, although awake and conscious, I was physically unable to make a movement. Invariably in such moments the mind veers off at a tangent and fastens onto some improbable occurrence; suppose, I thought, a thief should now enter the room and attack me; it would be too difficult for me to make any effort to protect myself.

How did it happen, I thought soggily, that I was on my bed in tennis clothes, in the darkness, with a fur rug over me? Why was I so leaden, so benumbed?

Then, as always, as my mind came alive, I thought of you. There was, I realized, something special I must review. Becoming increasingly awake, I struggled to grasp what it was, but, probably because some subconscious censor prohibited any frightening awareness, what I should think about eluded me. I forced my mind, bit by bit, into activity, possibly in protest against my sluggish body that lay like so much deadweight on the bed. Sleep fought to conquer me, and my tired body yearned for it. My right leg, doubled up under me, caused me a dull pain but I was too fatigued to move it.

The broken vase, I remembered suddenly and lucidly; you had left town, you were in the south; the *weather,* how was the weather? I must find out at once what kind of weather we were having. Under the impulse of strain and excitement I turned my head slowly towards the window; the thin voile curtains fluttered in cold gusts of wintry air; beyond, I saw the chill pinpoints of the stars flickering in the clear night. There was a great uncanny luminousness to the heavens; it was full moon. Cold, cold, came the air to me across the room; I could smell the cold as I breathed it and at the same time feel the waves of heat emanating from my sheltered body beneath the fur rug. I compared myself to one of those chaud-froid desserts served in expensive restaurants, a baked Alaska in reverse. The cold stung me slightly. I relaxed my aching, heavy head on the pillow, keeping my nose out of the protecting warmth of the fur as dogs do when they curl up like embryos on freezing nights. The window remained in my range of vision and I opened and closed my eyes in a slow winking. Because it was moonlight here did not mean it was an equally clear night in the south. At this time of year the south was racked by storms; but if it was cold here, it was colder there. The stars fizzled and blinked in the frame of the window.

We had once seen together, you and I, a primitive Italian painting with just such chill, distant, unreal stars. The picture had shown the roofless piazza of some nobleman's palace, jammed with a gathering of bright-hued brocade-gowned women in towering conical headgear and gaudily dressed, velveted men. We had commented on the contrast of the cold, white marble architecture against the soft fabrics of the dresses and suits of the men and the incredibly brilliant, unrealistic stars set in their somber blue against the warm sparkle of wines and fruits that focused attention on the center of the painting. How much we had done together, I thought sentimentally, how many pages of comment we had made on what we had seen or read or heard; or, more accurately, I thought with less sentimentality and more truthfulness, how much of my comments and criticisms you had stolen to appropriate as your own. My heart throbbed disagreeably, and a strange sound, or cacophony of sounds, swelled through it, ranging from dim, ominous drumming and thunderous hammerbeats to a shrill mosquito whining.

Was I now part of the painting itself, looking up at the stars from the courtyard of the piazza, or was I in my well-roofed house, on my bed?

A light, giddy feeling enveloped my head, disembodying it momentarily from my heavy body. My unaccustomed debauch was exacting quite a price. I drifted into a kind of waking sleep, not actually dreaming, yet not purposefully thinking, either, half-imagining, yet imagining distortedly, as in dreams, but not yet too distortedly to contradict reality.

It was night and you were in the snow. You had climbed high to reach some acceptable summit that would tax the efforts of the hunting party and further delay their search, for of course in the end there would be a search for you and you would be found and brought back to the fashionable hotel, a well-preserved, handsome corpse, frozen like so much meat, clean and odorless as if you had come out of a deep-freezer.

What was it we had once said about bodies and deep-freezers? Yes, we had invented, one summer Sunday afternoon as we had lounged about the swimming-pool, a business-of-the-future. We would open a concern for freezing people for desired lengths of time, charging specific but rather stiff fees, unfreezing them whenever their contracts with us terminated. In time of war, we had decided the Government would have the right to unfreeze all or any of our clients for enlistment in the armed forces. You had pointed out that in a business as delicate as freezing and defreezing we would need a crop of lawyers, for a woman who disliked her husband could arrange to have him delivered to us in a drunken stupor for freezement for any time from three days to thirty years; all that was required was that she pay the bill. I had decided our clients must pay their bills personally, half before freezing, the remaining half upon defreezement, and that no client could be accepted unless he were in full possession of his mental faculties. You had voted for a staff of psychiatrists, too; you had drawn a vivid picture of the maladjustments of a client frozen for several generations awakening into a strange, unknown world with no conditioning to make it intelligible to him, without friends except those who had chosen to be frozen with him, with outmoded clothes and no knowledge of the changes that had taken place in his town or city. I remember saying that the women would need special psychiatric attention for I claimed all women would want to be frozen for a decade at least between their fortieth and forty-fifth years and would prefer to return to the world a year at a time every ten years, thereby having the satisfaction of becoming younger than any unfortunate sisters who could not pay our fancy fees and having the advantage at the same time of hooking men by displaying a certain old-world charm that might be captivating in the new decade. And people with incompatible ages, you had said, could catch up with each other in our freezing plant, and then you had stopped, confronted with the wide difference between your age and mine. By my own estimation of my sex, I would have been frozen already at the time I met you.

You had made yourself as comfortable as possible in the snow, sheltered from any molesting wind, facing downhill. You had lost one ski in falling over a hidden boulder; the other ski jutted out from under you at an odd angle because of the unnatural position of your smashed right knee. You lay on your side propped on your elbow to take the weight off your mangled leg. The cold, mercifully, killed the pain. Perhaps, as I, you were surveying the clear heavens; perhaps you wondered what I might be thinking. Possibly,

240

deceived by the peace and stillness of the skies you even attempted to talk to me, but I doubted that. What more had you to say to me than what you had already told me? You grew stiff and cramped and ached a bit and then no doubt the welcome numbness began to seep through your body and the satisfying drowsiness came to claim you. Like a patient undergoing an anaesthetic, you hoped it would not wear off before the results you wished had been obtained. Were you at peace with me?

Far easier to be the painting, I thought, and endure forever without the worry and fret of disintegrating and stinking or of freezing and missing the present.

Did you like the snow? Except for a remark of mine on snowflakes and a comment of yours on the stooge's ski-ing we had never, before our last conversation together, talked of the snow. Once in my library we had come across a book of old Chinese landscapes and we had observed how wild and jagged the snow in the Chinese snowscapes appeared. You had called it "T'ang snow" after the period of the painters. Then we had looked through the Flemish folios until we found some Breughel snow-scenes and I had observed that Dutch snow seemed to be smoother, more polished and a good deal more tractable than Chinese snow. But that had hardly been a discussion of snow; we had been more concerned over painting techniques.

Did the old Italian lords and ladies nibbling at fruits in an open piazza under so chill a sky never shiver? Perhaps shivering had been considered a social offence, a disparagement on how the host had arranged the weather. Shiver is a foolish word; one shivers with cold, with fear, with pleasure, with heat.

Hear, I thought as the mosquito whining mounted higher in my ears, heat and cold are both extremes and extremes are supposedly similar. However, I should rather freeze than burn, although, heretic that I am, burning is, I suppose, more conventional for me. Witches burn; witches are women. What, then, freezes? Who freezes? Meat freezes; men are meat.

On your cold mountain top, did you perhaps allow yourself the luxury of considering the warmer episodes of your past with me? Did you perhaps dwell upon the hours we had spent together away from the city in a small, hilly village where we had met over weekends, each arriving separately like the most romantic lovers in Byronic poetry? The techniques by which lovers meet are always similar; a bit sly, devious, and by the very prohibition of the meeting add relish and value to the time together. Never being discovered, our childish enjoyment over our deceit had waned with the repeated successful executions of such stolen meetings. On the occasion I remember, we had tramped far into the low hills, entered the woods and spread our blanket in a patch of sunlight. Lying there together, you had told me that I smelled of the sun, not *like* the sun, but *of* it, and I had put my arm against my nostrils to sniff my skin; there had been a warm, sweet perfume, and I had turned to you and grazed my nose over your chest and belly and had found that you, too, smelled of the sun, warm and clean and even fiery. That autumn sun had tanned us gently, toasting us carefully without making us uncomfortable; it had been exciting in its heat and had soothed us after exciting us, and it had bathed us lavishly in the rarest perfume of the world, the scent of each other's bodies. In a way, we had been the sun itself that afternoon, of it and in it and like it. Heat made possible the fullest expression of living, and the sun was the most persuasive agent to render us conscious of living.

Was then the opposite true? Was cold the fullest expression of death and absence of sun—darkness itself—the most persuasive agent to make ourselves unconscious?

"Beloved, you smell of the sun," you had said to me, and your voice had been the delighted voice of the child who makes a thrilling and agreeable discovery. You had been the first to smell the sun. Does the cold smell? Does the snow?

"And all your body is warm and smooth," you had said, which had struck me as a juggling of some well-known phrase; later, I remembered that the conventional association of the words were *"cold* and smooth" and the comparison was, as a rule, *marble*. Cold and smooth are the dead, of course; warm and smooth is a lover's juxtaposition and unconscious protest against a force stronger than love.

In the warmth, we move and create; in the cold, in the cold, I thought desperately as I lay on the bed, what is it we do in the cold? But instead of an answer slipping into my mind, there entered a series of related words: cold, bold, hold, sold.

Had you been insufficiently bold in your relationship with me, or had I been overly so? Did I secretly resent the hold you had over me through your physical proximity? Did I suspect that you were willing to be sold to me in return for my fortune and advancement in the business? My fortune would increase as I grew older; it was cumulative; very likely my boldness would also increase as age made the obtaining of certain youthful pleasures more difficult for me. Could the word *hold* denote the tricks and subterfuges I would undertake to tie securely to me in the future those people I valued? Significantly, all these words—cold, bold, hold, sold—held within themselves that other word I so much disliked, *old*. Was I then so afraid of ageing? Or was I afraid that through ageing I would indubitably lose you and therefore I had taken such a circuitous, complicated method to be rid of you without undergoing the humiliation of losing you.

All the women in the Italian primitive were young. On the whole, painters—like any man—prefer young women. Aged people are curiosities. If they are men, they might conceivably and in rare cases be revered, but if they are women they are pushed aside. "Old and wise" is what is said of men; "old and ugly" is what is said of women.

In the Italian painting there had been squares of black and white marble patterning the courtyard. I wondered if that could be a primitive symbolism for life and death or were both symbols of death? When children die the biers are white, when adults die the biers are black. What was it you had said about white? I squeezed my eyelids in an effort of concentration. You had called white a color of death, the bride's dress being the virgin's shroud.

The Ming vase had been blue-white and smooth and cold;

were things what they appeared to be, was the vase just a vase and nothing more, or was it a symbol of something bigger, for example, of a dead love, a dead life? In brief, was it suicide you had committed, as it seemed, or would it be known there lay murder behind the appearances? But who was capable of penetrating behind the appearances? Who wished to? It was hardly unreasonable of me to suppose that in a world wherein we lived rather by appearances than by truth no one should care to deviate from the comfortable path of observing appearances and accepting what *seemed* for what *is*.

When I fell into a deep, black sleep I dreamt of you. I saw you a tiny, minuscule, humped-up figure dressed in brilliant hues seated at the extreme end of a long, dark hall, alone and aloof, hugging your knees. Around you there flew a conglomeration of dimly familiar sports equipment, limp tennis rackets and skis, graceful and quite pretty. In my dream I did not know whether the figure was really you or a painting of you and I had not the will to walk down the velvety passage and find out.

It was almost noon when I awoke and well towards two o'clock before I emerged from my slow dressing and bathing to find a flurry of telephone messages on my desk requesting me to call the old lawyer at once. So, I thought, fondling the white slips, it is already over, the advance news has reached town and soon the newspapers will publish the story.

"But I'm afraid something really serious has happened to him," the old lawyer insisted into the telephone after he had inquired after my health and explained to me that you had disappeared from the hotel.

"What on earth could have happened to him?" I asked crossly. "He's an excellent skier and he probably took a long trip by himself."

"Well, if he had an accident," the old lawyer explained, unable to guess I was misinterpreting deliberately, "he could have frozen to death. After all, that's wild country down there, and staying out overnight in below zero weather is apt to be fatal."

"Frozen to death!" I snapped at the old man. "Are you serious? And why should he have had an accident?"

"I tell you, my dear, I expect the worst. The worst." By the old lawyer's voice I could tell that, despite himself, he felt your death a very happy solution to the problem of what he should do with you in the firm.

"But that's horrible! What a frightening idea! Will you keep me informed? What are you doing about it?" I exclaimed and asked. To myself, I sounded most convincing.

I was trying to sit by the telephone and feign interest and worry as the old man called me every half-hour. The effort of constant dissembling tired me. It was over, it was over, I told myself repeatedly. Soon they would discover it for themselves. An unexpected snowstorm held up the searching-party and I was obliged to sit up deep into the night. I was thankful that, at least, I could receive the bulletins by telephone and not be hampered by the presence of anyone else in the room with me.

You had gone out alone the previous morning, which had

been cold and overcast but had in no way diminished the enthusiasm of the skiers. Most of them, however, had returned to the hotel in the early afternoon. Although you did not return at all during the night, nobody had missed you until this morning when a young man, claiming to be a close friend of yours (the stooge, of course), reported your absence. Other hotels were searched, as well as various bars and teashops, and finally a professional searching-party had set out into the mountains to find you. The progress of the party was radioed to the hotel which in turn telephoned it to the old lawyer who then telephoned me.

It was past midnight when the final telephone call came; I could tell at once by the old lawyer's hushed, awed tones that you had been found and that the aroma of death was seeping along the telephone wire. I endeavored to sound disbelieving, then shocked, then tearful. After the expression of suitable sentiments from both sides the old lawyer made a slip.

"I'll have to look into his papers. So far as I know he died intestate. *That* will be a nuisance." And then (I could almost hear him clamp his teeth over his cigar) recovering from this frank outburst he changed his tone back to that distant, respectful voice we invariably assume when we speak of the recently dead: "What a pity to die so young."

"What's being done about the body?" I asked.

There was a pause and then the old lawyer in a somewhat embarrassed voice explained to me that you were being buried in the little village near the ski-ing hotel because nobody had specifically asked that you be buried elsewhere and the expense of freighting a body for four days in a train was enormous, although the lawyer complained he found it illogical that a dead body should cost triple the transport charges of a live one. And the planes wouldn't handle a corpse.

"And the family?" I pressed.

"I'm cabling the family," the old lawyer said. "What's left of it. After all, it's only a short while since his father died. And I'll ship up to them all his belongings. I hope I find a will or somebody who knows whether he ever made a will. Lawyers and lawyers' assistants are always the people who never have time to get around to their own wills, they're so busy probating other people's wills." He sounded cross and tired, and I hung up the receiver, cutting short any further complaints.

It struck me as ironical that my first notice of your death should be a complaining one. Apparently you were a trouble-maker dead as well as alive.

The morning newspapers featured the tragedy with pictures. FRIEND FINDS BACHELOR'S BODY I read, and below a blown-up, foggy photograph of you was a smaller one of the friend, and I recognized the stooge's face. The faithful friend, I thought sourly, like a good old dog, loyal unto death. I read through the accounts of your arrival, your starting out on the ski-trip with other skiers, your absence, the search for you and the finding of your frozen body with its mutilated leg in a precipice on a far mountain. The national ski-champion, who claimed to be your closest friend, had risked "life and limb," in the journalese phrase, in his haste to find you.

It had been easy to reconstruct what had happened to you
for the evidence spoke eloquently. You had climbed so high
that the storm which had impeded the original efforts of the
searching-party apparently had been below you on the capa-
cious mountain-bosom. In the deceiving night-light, such as
it had been, you obviously had not seen the jagged rock and
had fallen on it, losing your left ski and crashing your right
knee against the enveloping ice and granite, disabling yourself. Unavoidably on this dangerous height in only night-
light a climber must meet with disaster. The accident was
in no way extraordinary; what was extraordinary was your
having obtained such an altitude at all in almost total darkness, avoiding—by what miracle could only be surmised—
the fatal glacier-crevices far below. You had dragged yourself
to the lee of the rock and reclined in the snow very much in
the position of a Roman senator at a banquet.

I sent out for additional morning papers to glean further
details but all the reporters had told the same story in different words. There was no mention of the novia; perhaps
the honeymoon angle of the affair was being held back for
the evening editions to make the story retain public interest
a bit longer.

Without exception, all the papers speculated on what
could have induced you to undertake such a climb. The
tabloids referred to it, luridly enough, as a "death-climb,"
pointing out you had struck out for a height ordinarily attempted only by specially equipped expeditions and, conse-
quently, your intention must have been to slog upward
until you fell from exhaustion. The solider, more established

249

papers maintained there could be no conceivable suicide-motive behind your climb and pointed out that in Europe such heights were frequently scaled by excellent skiers with little difficulty. Of course there was a certain pointlessness to your exploit, but this was tactfully counteracted by a history of your previous ski-audacities (all of them news to me, and I suspected the penny-a-line reporter had invented them, for your natural conceit would never have hidden from me such astounding and agile feats of prowess). The casual reader gained an impression of a wild, reckless young bachelor rushing off into the night on a mad ski-trip and meeting with a fatal accident which was a kind of fitting, tragic climax to an adventurous life.

Recalling your fantastic gyrations on our bicycle ride years ago when you had flirted with death out of sheer high spirits, I thought perhaps that this crazy climb of yours had been provoked by a macabre display of superhuman strength and stamina, which might be termed a morbid expression of high spirits. That you had had a possible accident, however, disturbed me. I was certain that was something you had not bargained for. This accident, for it *seemed* an accident, robbed me of the final certainty of my responsibility. Had you committed suicide to the satisfaction of the coroner I would have had no doubts at all; I would have known the responsibility for your death was as surely mine as if I had shot you. Had your climb been a "death-climb" or had you wanted nothing more than a temporary escape, an illusion of freedom and aloneness? If it had been a death-climb then the accident had forestalled your suicide and I had not, actually, suc-

ceeded with the execution of my crime; chance had inter-
vened. In addition, there was always the possibility you had
not considered killing yourself at all and were as protesting
against death as most of us. But that did not tally with your
talks to me and with the fact that you apparently had resigned yourself at once to the fatality of your position. Although I knew I was behind your death (but was I?), although I *thought* I was behind your death, I could not prove
it to myself. Because of the accident I could not know, could
not deduce in what frame of mind you had set out on your
climb.

Accident or suicide, my plan had been realized and I am
not one to be concerned over the means to an end. It is the
end that counts.

Having read of criminals who collected the newspaper
clippings recounting their crimes, I deliberately threw the
newspapers into the fireplace as usual. I had the impression
that what was published in the papers was unreal, had nothing whatsoever to do with you, was, in fact, a reportage of
an unknown person. I was tempted to tell myself the old
story with which people seek to hypnotize themselves: *He
has gone away for a short time.* Instead, I told myself you
were dead, dead, dead until the word had no meaning for
me and I was saying my phrase automatically, thinking,
meanwhile, of other things. The truth was I wanted to make
myself believe that my crime was actually not committed. I
had thought so frequently of your death that now that it
had occurred it already seemed something that had happened a long time ago, *while you were still living.*

The old lawyer telephoned me requesting me to come to your apartment to determine if there was anything of yours I would like to have as a memento and, incidentally, by taking it save him the trouble of shipping it to your family. You had died without leaving a will and your closest kin was entitled to all your belongings, that is, your mother. I refused to go to your flat; I claimed your death had upset me and I couldn't face an ordeal. In reality, I did not want to see your flat being disbanded, stripped.

"But his books," the old lawyer begged into the telephone. "How can I ship his books up? They're books bought here. What possible interest could his mother have in those?"

I objected I had no place for your books. I wanted no reminders of you. I suggested the books be given to the seamen's mission or to a public library.

The old lawyer agreed, reluctantly, that that was a sensible idea and proceeded to discuss your furniture with me.

"Sell it to an auction house," I recommended, wondering if the novia would attempt to claim any of it.

"That leaves only the clothes and personal articles to send off," the old lawyer enumerated, "and some old letters, mostly girl-friends'." I wondered, in a moment of panic, if any of mine might be among them, and then concluded you would not have been sufficiently vindictive to cause me such inconvenience. "And a picture, a Bolivian primitive, not bad. Wouldn't you like it?" the old lawyer asked me, and I knew, from his inflection, that he wanted it.

I declined and said I was sure you would want him to

have something of yours and the picture was just the thing. The old lawyer quickly agreed with me.

So, over the telephone, impersonal and removed, I managed the disposal of those articles you had gathered together as evidence of the sort of man you were and the kind of life you had lived. I avoided all contact with your belongings. I dispersed the symbols that stood for your tastes, your habits and yourself.

As I had expected, the evening papers carried an amplification of the story and brought out into the spotlight the tragedy of the stooge's discovering his best friend's body while honeymooning. A picture of the stooge and the novia and you, like three convicts taken in profile, topped the headlines in a photographic strip.

When asked [I read the account of the interview with the novia] if she could conceive of any reason why so handsome and successful a young man could want to risk his life in a lonely ski-trip, the lovely newlywed shook her dark curls and replied: "It's all a complete mystery to me."

After this article I ceased reading the newspapers; such accounts were cheapening and vulgar. Friends telephoned me to discuss your death with the same enjoyment that housewives comment on unusual recipes. I moved in an imitation of myself and my doings, but nobody seemed to realize I was in any way different from normal. I even overheard comments that I certainly wasn't much affected by your death.

The telephone calls and visits and newspaper comments

ceased and after the four days' attention you were forgotten. It was then that you became real to me and I began to understand what I had done. I began to prepare myself to live without you.

Remorse is an indication of incapacity; one is only sorry for what one could have done differently, and since I had planned for your death (presumably because I wanted you to die) I could not permit myself the weakness of remorse. My ends were won, why should I fret over the means of their execution, or even the fact that finally I had executed my plans? Was not this a cause for satisfaction?

Perhaps this is how things should have been, perhaps this is what I had pretended was possible, a rejoicing because of my victory over you, a celebration because I had triumphed, had been in this, as in everything else in my life, entirely successful.

It is no use. I have nothing to think about that keeps me alive. My mind is a dreary realm that lacks a sovereign. It is as if, like some medieval queen, I sallied forth to battle against my arch-enemy, a local neighboring king, and, having won against him, I return to my castle only to discover that my lords and ladies and vassals and hunting dogs and falcons are unsatisfactory ghosts and my real raison d'être has been the war I waged. There are natures in this world which are at harmony with themselves only when engaged in a specific activity; such a nature, I discovered, is my own, and the activity has been my campaign against you.

I am frightened as I become increasingly aware of what it means never to see you again, never to watch you enter

my house, nor to go to your apartment, and the enormity of
my loss is slowly making itself felt, saddening my very bones
so that I am lusterless and morose. The outward show that
I can still put on passes muster, but I know—and who else
now counts?—how dreary is my private life. Perhaps I love
you more now that you are beyond my reach. It is often said
that real love awakens only after the loss of the beloved.

The zest and excitement you brought with you when I
took you into my life has been eliminated. With the pall of
dullness settling over me I feel as if I am smothering in the
heavy swaddling blankets of old age.

My old lawyer complains of a lack of interest on my part
in the firm. Of course you were the cause of my close following of the business, I wanted to know what you did in
the office, I wanted to be able to discuss with you and ad-
vise you on business matters, as well as on all else. What
concern is the business to me now? It will plod on, a fairly
profitable enterprise, without both our efforts, turning out
dividends on its own momentum.

I am not seen at the concerts in the opera-house and I
have lied and said I am too busy to go. That's hardly true.
How can I go back, as to a trysting place, into the concert
hall where I know so well the plush-and-gilt and which I
associate so completely with you? What shall I do there,
you being absent? What's music to me if you cannot listen
to it? What's anywhere to me if you are not there?

I wonder that I ever played tennis. The racket lies heavy
in my hand and the court seems immense and soggy. I have
ceased to move with the elasticity required of even average

players so I leave the court to my younger guests and those clients that the old lawyer persistently brings around to be impressed by me, by my house, by my wealth.

Last week I passed the open door of the garage and saw my bicycle leaning against the wall, its tyres flat and the handlebars rusted with moisture. What trivial, inconsequential signs point to a change in a person. Of course I shall not cycle again. Who is worth such an effort? Who will examine me that closely again?

It is only a question of time before this inner destruction working below my skin will show its effects and everyone will see that I am, after all, an elderly woman. I have thought of marrying again, perhaps the old lawyer himself as a sort of final social triumph for him, but how shall I put up with a spent old man when I have known the resiliency of your youth?

I have destroyed you as I set out to do. I could not know that in destroying you instead of preserving myself I was also destroying myself. I am not foolish enough to follow you, I will not show a defeat, I will live, as I once told you, because I am so curious, because living is so wonderful. Living was indeed most wonderful with you in my world, it is something quite hollow and distasteful without you.

If I have killed you, you have robbed me. I took your life and you have taken my youth. Perhaps I should put it differently. Perhaps I should say that when I killed you, you gave me something that was inescapably mine, something that you had been withholding from me, reserving for me: you gave me old age.